Forbidden And Unholy Speculations

Other Books by the Author

BLOOD FLOWER

ETMA PNIKRE

LOCK LINKED—INTELLIGENCE—INSTINCT—DREAMS—
EDUCATION

INTELLIGENCE and INSTINCTS
(UNDERSTANDING YOURSELF AND OTHERS)

JAGUAR and FIVE RABBIT

THE ASKANDAR

DREAMS
(The Real Truth)

Editor of—KALEIDOSCOPE ONE

Forbidden And Unholy Speculations

Norris Ray Peery

Writers Club Press
New York Lincoln Shanghai

Writers Club Press
an imprint of iUniverse, Inc.

For information address:
iUniverse
2021 Pine Lake Road, Suite 100
Lincoln, NE 68512
www.iuniverse.com

Front Cover Graphic is by the Author.
This print edition is Version: V-1.2

ISBN: 0-595-26269-4

Printed in the United States of America

For
those very special persons who have
Inquisitive
And
Hungry
Minds

Note: Whenever it is convenient, this book should be read aloud.

Contents

*   *   *

THE BEGINNING

THE MIND IS A MIRROR THAT HAS BEEN ETCHED WITH THE ASH OF WHAT ONCE WAS THE UNIVERSE.

Our world, its nations, their peoples, and we as individuals find that time and events have brought us once again to the edge of a political, economic, social, philosophical, and moral cliff. One step farther into the future we can see our possible plunge downward onto the rocks of hopeless despair, where anarchy reins in a landscape of unemployment, crime, and social injustice. A landscape where the best ideals of our kind,—Justice—Love—Kindness—and Hope for a better future—have vanished into the past, leaving only their ghosts to haunt the valleys of our sad dissolution.

How is it that governments, religions, and other institutions, and their peoples can stir the pot of life until they have it in such a turmoil of uncontrollable currents swirling and churning in each and every direction that almost no one understands exactly how or why things are, as they are, and brave and honest people back away from the chaos in despair.

Political liberals attempt to stir the fluxing brew with tools of good intent, but all of their dabs and dips into the swirling mass causes new uncontrollable currents to wax and wane and brings a torrent of bubbles of social injustice grumbling to the surface.

Political conservatives with a cocksure attitude rush to apply old and hopeless solutions to a turmoil they have never before seen. Like sorcerers they work an old ritual in precisely the same manner they had before seen their forefathers use to still troubled waters. This new swirling pot of despair takes no heed of their lovely dance, intricate and well intended as it may well be. The torrents of the pot rise up against each intended control and threaten to consume all who would apply old and weak magic.

Religious leaders cry-out the futility of even trying to understand what it is all about, and warn all to return to the religious sanctuary of ask nothing, think nothing, and do nothing. All that is necessary, they say, is to believe in their religious doctrine and all will be saved. A call they have been making to humankind since nature first gave them tongues and throats. Like parrots they have repeated, their never-ending, and never-changing message of impending doom and final salvation to each and every generation of our kind, claiming the end of all is at hand any moment, and this unheeded call of theirs has echoed down through the centuries, like the false cry of "Wolf" echoing off the walls of time's long and tormented passageway.

The very air of our time is ripe with emotions and fear, while believable leadership is nowhere to be found. Millions of voices of confused self-named leaders and followers flood the air with commands that lead in every direction, with finger pointing this way and that, while near to the heart of humankind on the throne of authority sits, the mannequin shell of what once was leadership. Somewhere on history's long and winding rock strewn path, in some crevasse forgotten by the masses as they marched on, leadership was pushed and disappeared. Now on that once hopeful throne, mannequins sit, and from this place of highest power, they act out a ritual of giving out gifts, hour, by hour. It matters little who sits on that throne, for the ways of leadership is to them all, unknown, it is lost in a crevice of the past. And as nations, and peoples beat their breasts in some unrecognized mourning, the greatest turmoil of all time begins its slow boil. Mannequins practicing giftmanship have not the slightest powers of true leadership, whose magic was to inspire, and whose right to sit on authority's throne, was not given, but recognized, and then honored by free choice.

The situation is such that most people know within their hearts the terrible solution history has repeatedly imposed as the final result of such a turmoil of purpose. No sane person can hope that our future will repeat the same heartless, inhuman, and tragically fatal consequences, we have witnessed in the historic past, as the sole means out of our present dilemmas.

We, each of us, must refuse to allow the "Old Philosophies," that crush the individual in the name of order to again be repeated as the solution to our problems. If we hope for better times, better ways to solve our problems, then we must understand exactly the nature of our real problems. We must see them, truthfully, squarely, and eye-to-eye. If we are willing to see the truth, as it stands naked before us, then we, with truth can find the answers, and there should not be the slightest doubt about this. It seems to be only the most obvious common sense that in seeking the solution to any problem, that you would like to know the truth of the matter as the first prerequisite. Without the prerequisite of truth, what hope do we have? Not all of the magic, or slight of hand, or hopeful words, or mystic ways based on deception, can ever give us salvation from anything, not even from ourselves.

We live in today's world, and it is a world where there is much to be understood. It is a world ultimately different from the world of even forty or fifty years ago. Within our world of today, we have time-cherished philosophies, whose basic axioms are no longer valid. Our cultures abound with philosophies that enshrine, not truth, but wanton lies. In our world of today, in many instances, we have some institutions whose ultimate purpose is to hide truth, and other institutions whose function is to create near human robots, robots designed to fit a sick slick culture's institutional and social molds. The ultimate product of our cultural institutions is named, "The Average Person." The average person is an animal so perfectly programmed, that they fit easily into statistical formulas that predict their almost every action. They are people who have had a systematic education, one that destroys almost all traits that would have allowed them to become an imaginative, creative, and supremely unique individual. There is not one of us who has completely escaped the partial destruction of our potential abilities that cultures and their institutions have worked upon our brains. We, each of us, walk through life as partially mentally crippled individuals, and we owe this handicap, that each of us bear, to our cultures and their institutions, whose philosophies have not kept pace with our kind's expanding knowledge of the Creator God's nature and of our true place within creation.

We live in a world filled with vast hypocrisies and where the most massive of lies are decorated with sparkling glitter and hang suspended, above our heads, by threads of faith whose only strength is found within their numbers.

We live in a world where the grossest absurdities stand daily before our eyes, and we see them not. We live in a world where the contrast, between truth and the lie, is like night and day, and we see it not. The human animal does not see the world by the eye, but by means of the brain, and our brains have been made blind and insensitive to any truth that tells a bitter story. But to ignore truth, is every person's, every culture's, and every nation's, sure and certain path towards a final destruction.

Our world of today is a world of paradoxes grown so large, that they are ready to explode, ready to devastate our social fabric and render it twisted beyond hopeful repair. We must try to understand, that the forces that ultimately destroyed the great civilizations of the past, were not marching armies, or man-made machines that exploded cities, but simply, humankind's unwillingness to understand truths that are far more powerful than powders, potions, swords of steel, or the mightiest of marching armies.

What problems are there that sit so very near to the heart of human kind, that we see them not? For time immemorial, people of a common language have struggled to communicate their hopes, dreams, and fears, history has been the sad placard of their failure, but time has made this immedicable failure the terminal cancer of our present world. It is true that the gulf representing the extremes of the intellectual spectrum, which separates peoples within today's societies is so enormous, that most people of different intellectual backgrounds cannot successfully communicate with one another, even though they essentially share a common language. At no previous time in human history has such a huge communications gap existed between peoples of a common language. It is a bitter paradox that such a situation exists at a time, when we are surrounded with the most powerful tools for mass communication that the world has ever known. And from this one bitter seed, like some wanton misguided nightmare of evolution, has sprung a forest of tangled vine, that winds its way into every garden where our kind's sapling hopes are systematically strangled by it common presence. And woe be to those whose language is not common to our own, because between them and us, powerful misconceptions will drag us both like limp puppets towards inevitable quarrels and conflicts, which neither of us knowingly chose.

We hear in the air the angry voices of this or that faction, demanding that they be heard. All people cry-out some hope, some fear, some dream, begging to be heard, to be understood, and many a lovely song, a potent warning, a good dream, a bright idea, dies smothered under economic power's heavy foot. Those who communicate their ideas by means of the power of their numbers, cause their idea to rock like thunder and lightening across the landscape, but there it dies from lack of understanding, like some sudden showers, blown briefly across a summer's long monotonous face. **Many a fish shall perish. Many a machine shall rust. Many a howl of nature stilled, and many a garden shall become dust, until people can speak together, and understand.**

EDUCATION AND IGNORANCE

LOGIC IS A BASIC SPIRITUAL SUBSTANCE WHICH EXISTS IN ALL THINGS

Near to the heart of humankind sits, like some dinosaur from a landscape of time's past, our cherished educational systems. Draped in modern buildings and wearing flashy instruments and bangles and beads, the body of modern education still speaks with half the voice of ancient Egypt. Translated Egyptian hieroglyphics have a child pleading with his teacher, *"Don't beat me master, for I have learned my lessons well."* Every culture's god of learning is rote memorization, and it, together with the whip, make a time tested duality of power for forcing children into becoming women and men of culture's desired mold. It's a simple system of monotonous repetition and fear, whose final product is a most stunning reflection of the method itself. It's a system that mechanically tramples, strangles, and mutilates the most human of human traits, the desire to seek, discover, and learn. The desire for learning in the young human child is the bubbling fountain of their youth, its water pure curiosity, and its forceful drive far exceeds all else in the animal kingdom. But in every culture, we see the child's sparkling enthusiasm for learning, systematically crushed, crushed, and crushed, until learning has been turned from joy into drudgery, from seeking to accepting, and from understanding to parroting. The educational system, which we have hypocritically named "Modern", is the "Ancient System," where the whip has been replaced by other fears. It all results in the same end, and speaks with an archaic hollow voice, lacking in understanding, echoing up from the distant dark past, out of cadence with our time's demands.

Out from under the umbrella of modern education, ignorance in masquerade dances, waving certificates and declarations in distracting motions, while each foot makes little hidden kicks of death, and the lips and throat gargle out warnings disguised as song, whose hidden words prophesied, our culture doesn't have long. It's a threatening dance it makes; each stumble is disguised as grace. If the dance goes on too long, it may engulf the entire human race. More than half of all our kind, jig to the music of this tune, and what's stuffed inside their brains, is just hot air for the balloon. Hardly one word of truth rattles in their brains. They barely can figure out, where to catch their busses and trains. They've gone through life with blinders on each side, and they can't figure out, where, or why, education died. It's not by marching armies that civilizations stumble and fall, and where then its citizens live amongst the heaps of scrawl, and time passes them by whimpering in the past. It's the devil's dance of ignorance that gets them in the last.

We might think of the people of our world as something like Bonsai trees. We take the infant seed of our kind, and plant it in the narrow confining pots of our culture and its institutions, and there it produces dwarfed giants of what we could have been. We should rename the present human animal, and call it the Bonsai Primate. Our culture and some of its institutions do to the spirit and mind of our kind, what we have purposefully done to some trees, we have forced them into becoming dwarfs of what they could have been.

We are regrettably evermore becoming people who are unable to muster the mental prowess needed to follow and comprehend the long sequential strings of logic, which form the basic ingredients of much of the modern world. And we shy away from even trying to squeeze out an understanding from any subject whose logical depth takes any proportional effort to decipher. We are unwilling to seriously investigate any subject that cannot easily be summarized on the back of a breakfast cereal box. We become overly tired and extremely uncomfortable when challenged by any logic that is more than two levels deep. If we believe a subject might make us the least bit weary while trying to understand it, and out of knowing the weakness of our own logical structures, we leave those subjects to others. We leave any seemingly difficult thinking to others, who claim to be professional experts of the subject, and by this excuse we leave the matters of governments and of international politics solely to others. We have, by excusing ourselves from the intellectual pursuit of everything of any real logical substance, become a nation where multitudes of good and honest causes are sacrificed to the grossest of illogical ideas based solely upon our feelings, and great ideas are slaughtered by an ignorance which is personified within many of our peoples. We need to develop the logical structures of our mind into powerful tools that can see the truth of what exists in a world that is otherwise opaque. And to do this we only need to increasingly exercise the structures of our mind, by ever teething the mind upon more and more substantial sequences of connected logic, which lead to a final logical conclusion. If nothing else, our schools should be relentlessly exercising every student's natural logical abilities to comprehend ever longer logical structures, this is our only hope for finding salvation from a future world, where ignorance can become the shackles which restrict intellect and from where escape is just a dying dream. Simply by exercising our mind's natural logical structures they become daily more powerful, in a way equivalent to how the body's muscles become stronger and more powerful as they are systematically exercised against increasingly difficult tasks.

It is generally the case in today's world that for most persons who have been educated in a specific curriculum, when they are required to make something entirely new, they go about the task as if they see only the specific path they have been taught by their training to follow. They can only see one path. But the persons who are able to repeatedly deliver the totally new and imaginative breakthroughs, they are persons, who see not just the path, but they also see the overall landscape of the situation.

We have been warned by some doctrines that to seek the fruits of the tree of knowledge is a transgression against one of a god's original commandments, but this is a latent lie, and for us not to seek the fruits of the tree of knowledge is within itself one of the greatest transgressions that any creature can make against the God of Creation, it is one of the unforgivable transgressions.

Ignorance was at one time the mental disease of dark times past and of the distant village cultures, but it has become more prevalent throughout all lands, where it is now the mother and father of the thriving twin infants, unreasonable fear and unreasonable hatred. These twins now sinisterly stalk the world's best hopes for better tomorrows.

One of the primary causes of an intellectual and social collapse of nations is an ignorance which inevitably becomes a growing condition that finally engulfs the entire population, and one of the potent signs indicating the beginning of an unwholesome social decay, is not an increased prevalence in the practices of age old so-called sins of the body, but instead is embodied in an ever increasing diversion of the accepted meanings of the words of the nation's language, or languages, a kind of "Tower of Babel" consequence, where the exactness of logical meanings within the words become evermore subject to multitudes of possible meanings, some of which are contradictions of each other. It is a condition which gives rise to a situation of languages within languages, of babble within babble.

It should be axiomatic that it is ever important that a language change by evolving into becoming ever more exactly understood by all of a nation's citizens. Everyone should surely be able to understand the inevitable dire consequences of the situation, which develops when the exact opposite of this axiom thrives within any nation.

THE CONTAGIOUS POISONED MIND

THE STRANGLER OF OUR GESTATING SOUL

We are all of us biased about everything, and as a matter of fact, we can only see and understand the physical or philosophical world around us, or see any argument in terms of what we already know, and what we already believe. In the truest sense we are pointed to our future destiny by our past knowledge, and to travel in any different direction requires that we purposefully understand who, what, and where we are, and only then can we undertake the most difficult effort of making a self-change. So like some monumental mass whose inertia at the current moment determines its future course, our kind is caught up within a world of beliefs whose substance, whose mass, has been ever growing from an infant planted seed. A seed which was germinated eons ago by an ignorant hope of believing that some invisible magic could deliver us from our miseries, and so because we were falsely led to believe, we sold our sacred and most precious god given birthright to the darkest of all dark forces, for they claimed without evidence that they were the light, and then the beast from hell came forth into our midst forever disguised as the lamb. And so, as an inevitable consequence, monstrous lies grew from what was originally blind hope. Our most precious birthright "Reason" we vowed to ignore, and agreed to substitute in its place "Blind Faith," blind faith in a promised magic that we could not see, smell, taste, hear, or feel with our god given minds and bodies. And so a new incurable plague settled upon our kind's minds, a plague with little hope for any logical cure.

This monstrous plague of humankind, "The Contagious Poisoned Mind," has been with us throughout all of time. It is stronger than any viral or bacterial infection. There are no known cures. The plague's symptoms are oftentimes hidden, and oftentimes more disastrously apparent than any pox that has ever made it mark upon our kind. No person has ever been born with this disease, but early in life it can infect the body, and its infection finally creeps to the very seat of the soul, were it is able to skew and twist rational thought into an ugly preconceived thing, a disguised monster who gaily dances a mesmerizing dance across life's stage. The plague most times does not murder the body, but lies waiting in its harbor, from where it works its poisons against the mind, poisons which are set certain to destroy, joy, pleasure, and to cripple the children of the mind, and to blind the mind's eye to the hopeful promises held by the future. This disease is born of that for which it is meant to destroy, and disguises itself with emptiness, thus making it invisible, hidden in this way, it walks with humankind through the centuries, sure to greet us at every door of time's passage. Haunting, mocking, ugliest of all things, hidden in the guise of pure truth and beauty, this plague rises up from every passageway of time, where it stands against every hope, against every dream, against the nature of the Creator God's universe itself, while it destroys, mutilates, and rejoices in a celebration of its own unhindered continuance.

What evil destroyers humankind has with patience finally purged from the body, Polio, Leprosy, Syphilis, and Smallpox, the list goes on and on, but the disease of the contagious poisoned mind is so hidden that it has not met the documentation of medical textbooks. Humankind is afraid to name this monster among us, as a true mental disease, and so it is allowed to continue its sickness and freely spread its plague forward in time without medical or any determined effort to stop its spread.

Adults, those who are already carriers of the contagious poisoned mind's disease, spread the disease by slowly introducing it to very young minds, minds that have not yet reached the temple of individual reason, the carriers of the disease feed to adolescent minds their ancient primitive rules of blackest magic, which have been disguised as the guiding light. They bait the young minds with promises that when their ancient illogical rules are followed, their magic will yield up the keys for opening the gates of the stairway, which leads to heaven. And they solemnly declare that if their magic rules are not followed, the worst of hells, will for eternal time, fall upon their young heads. By this path of slowly poisoning the young minds during their most susceptible time, their time of childhood innocents, the most unreasonable and completely illogical beliefs are taught to be worshipped as sacred, as holy ideas, ideas passed up from the dark places of some distant past, a past where ignorance was the most common name. We are asked to believe that although ignorance was that time's name, the god or gods of all of creation were drawn to speak face-to-face with these ancient peoples, and to give to them the black magic rules for salvation from their own ancient god's handmade traps. And the biases and hatreds, against those whose beliefs are different from theirs, are passed from one generation to the next in a nearly unbroken chain that connects a primitive, ancient, ignorant dark past to the present day. The poisons of the disease are dripped slowly, and uninhibited, into the vessels of the sensitive unresistive young minds. The disease has a very long gestation period, and grows only slowly within a young mind, but given time, and repeated inoculations of the poisonous and illogical beliefs, any young mind can eventually be permanently poisoned to see the world and its individuals in terms of blind and unreasonable misconceptions. And the vessels of their minds are filled with a hatred for those who hold different beliefs. And they have hatred for other persons, which they have been systematically poisoned against.

And we see that those who have poisoned minds are willing to stand to their death for totally unreasonable ideas, which are purported to be sacred, claiming god's purpose as their banner of martyrdom, but those same persons wouldn't dare risk even a harsh word as a wound for standing for what is actually morally right, good, and true. They are willing to even cut their own throat, as it is metaphorically said, and bathe in the hypocrisy of the illogical purpose for which it was done.

We can see the results of the contagious poisoned mind in every demonstration of an illogical hatred that is directed towards certain groups or individuals, which are in someway seen as being marked differently from the hater. We see how individuals and groups who have been infected with the contagious poisoned mind, apply their unreasonable hatred against individuals who have a different shade of skin color, a different religious conviction, a different style of speaking, a different sexual orientation, a different ethnic background, a different political philosophy, or any trait that they might conceive as marking another individual, as truly an individual who is different from them. We can see in these days, those with contagious poisoned minds willingly, and with an ignorant disregard for the lives of others, sacrifice their befuddled and confused lives in what they believe is a holy obligation to destroy by murder the innocent lives of their self appointed enemies. And they execute these crimes, against innocent peoples, directed by their holy faith in a preposterous and poisoned lie, which declares, they will receive some holy reward for their disgusting lack of intellect, and their willingness to follow the ravings of another's contagious poisoned mind, another righteous fool's blind ravings of a secrete divine purpose and the fulfillment of some flimsy prophesy.

We should not be at all surprised, that the primary sources, for distributing the infection of the contagious poisoned mind, are in many cases considered to be sacred holy sanctuaries within every society. Some of those sanctuaries are most times accepted and well respected institutions that have maintained their dominance within the social structure by the very means of propagating an endless army of persons, who have contagious poisoned minds, and who are therefore willing, without considerate thought, and unable to call on reason, to engage in the continued propagation of beliefs and hatreds, which are clearly without any intellectual merit whatsoever. The saddest part of this story, is that the respected institutions have no other means whatsoever of maintaining their position of authority and power within a society without resorting to being the primary source for ever propagating contagious poisoned minds. Sadder yet, is the army of their believers with contagious poisoned minds, who willingly bring their children to the altars of these respected institutions, altars, where the Creator God's gift of reason is sacrificed to the invisible idol gods of the contagious poisoned mind. And even sadder, is the undeniable fact that the greatest gift that the God of the Universe bestowed upon any of god's creatures, is the most sacred, the most holy gift of all, the gift of logical reasoning, and any institution, group, or individual, who would deny an individual's freedom and god given right to use this sacred gift of logical reason, is without doubt committing the ultimate crime against creation's God, and that God's most precious gift to humankind, and this is the supreme crime, the ever unforgivable crime against god and the most holy of gifts from the Great Creator God of the Universe. There are no excuses of any kind, from any source, which can justify this unholy crime against the ultimate kind of prophetic vision, which only the gift of logical reasoning bestows upon our kind. No ignorance dressed in golden costumes and performing ritual movements, can give any truthful substance to the evil sickness, which professes "Faith" supreme over "Reason." This crime can no longer be hidden behind the clouds of sweet incense smoke billowing up within the towering sculpted rock buildings that are falsely named, "Temples of God." No devised magnificent rituals, no great chanting choruses, no pageants of faith of any kind should any longer be allowed to be the camouflaging curtain, which hides this unholy crime against reason, reason which is the ultimate divine ethereal substance of god's natural evolution, and is our kind's bright shining visionary light, our only true prophetic light, which offers us some insight and guidance to a better future.

There are many reservoirs within societies that are willing repositories and propagators of contagious poisoned minds. It is within some families that many of the worst biases and hatreds against some groups or individuals are succored and nurtured, as if they needed protection, and are passed from an adult's mouth to a child's ear, or by an adult's actions to a child's viewing, and in this way the poisons, from one contagious poisoned mind, are passed from one generation to the next.

In our world and time, tens of thousands of our young men and women, who have been most poisoned and have a contagious poisoned mind, are sent out into the nation's of world, where they willingly and with a most sincere belief that they are doing some god's holy work, willingly and ignorantly spread the most unholy of lies, which are the invisible seeds from which grow new contagious poisoned minds, and this disease, which they joyfully spread, increasingly strangles with ancient cords, braided from the trinity of forbid, forbid, and forbid, human kind's best hopes for an ever growing knowledge and forever better tomorrows.

For how much more time are we willing to allow this dead and rotting horse to be ridden through our cultures as if it represented truth in all its magnificent glory?

OUR TRAIL THROUGH THE PAST'S HELL

LIFE IS ALL THERE IS OF HEAVENS OR HELLS

After tens of thousands of years, during which times our ancestors worshiped at the shines of false idol gods and invisible spirit gods, we can finally see, with understanding eyes, our true historical trail as it suffered its meandering journey through our ancient and primitive past. We can finally understand that our proven historical past was a time and place, which was nearly joyless and mostly filled with pain and terrible sufferings, it represents an epic tale of our relentless struggle to survive within nature's unforgiving and savagely hostile environment. It was a time when we stumbled through an intellectual darkness, which was blacker than any night, a time where we blindly bumped into every pitfall of an ornery uncaring nature, and out of our shear and nearly hopeless desperation for survival, we grasped blindly at any and every possibility that seemed to offer even the slimmest glimmer of hope for delivering us from that place and time of hell.

We must here consider matters, which are considered to be taboo and forbidden for discussion. Religion is a phenomenon that is common in one form or another to all cultures throughout all of conscious human time. It should be very much to our interest as to what this commonality is all about. It should not be difficult to understand, in the course of the slow emergence by means of the natural evolution of the biological mechanisms of human intelligence, that our kind was also slowly beginning to see their world in new and very different terms, than they had ever before known. They were beginning to see their world as filled with much, which was to their young evolving intelligence, incomprehensible in terms of any observable natural cause and effect, and they saw everywhere mystery driven by hidden forces. And so, along with the slow emergence of human intelligence, another invisible ethereal creature slowly began evolving within our primitive minds, and that creature was religion, a creature who only worships at the shrines of ignorance and of unknown things, and whose natural mother is Ignorance, and whose natural father is Fear. Its father and mother have been and are common to every culture of every time. Religion is the ethereal creature whose only means of surviving through time is the milk it forever suckles from both of its immortal parents.

We are a people obsessed with believing, at nearly any cost, the unbelievable, if it contains even the slightest promise of salvation from our miseries, or of our escaping from death. We are a people willing to sacrifice whatever is requested by false prophets, who claim to personally know and to personally represent some god's desire.

For tens of thousands of years we have been burying our kind within the bosom of Mother Earth. Promises of life renewed are offered over our graves, promises, which are guaranteed to be true by magical ceremonies performed over the lifeless bodies. All this cheep theatrical religious black magic and hocus pocus, which has changed and evolved throughout the centuries has proven itself to be nothing more than a hoax perpetrated on an ignorant and brain-washed public, who in their desperation are willing to believe anything, anything at all, which promises that our beloved family members and our friends will not forever parish from this world. But all the religious magic, though it has changed again-and-again during the passage of many centuries, has no power to deliver on its false promises, and our beloved ones are for evermore lost because we have been naively willing to believe in the false promises of some magical deliverance and resurrection. A resurrection that conveniently always lies in some far distant future, and where the reality of the false promise is forever hidden. By this method, those who are ever instigating cleaver new false religious magic, and who are never discovered to be the power hungry immoral charlatans that they actually are, continue to have multitudes of followers who are required to bear a testimony of their unshakeable faith in the truth of the fake magic and of the whole illusionary religious world that the charlatans have painstakingly woven around their follower's numbed minds.

There would seem to be a more realistic and surely a much more fruitful and rewarding approach than is this "faith" in the supposed religious magic, whose claim is to guarantee our survival beyond death. If we are foolish enough to continue to have "faith," and believe, while at the same time we continue to bury our loved ones in the Earth, or to offer up their bodies in funeral fires to the blue skies above, then we certainly, without any doubt, deserve the only proven end result of such actions, results we can clearly see this false magic delivers. But, if we are wise enough to say—not surely—not without any doubts—but maybe—this religious magic might be—just might possibly be false, then how might we better proceed? What numerous new pathways of real hope have been opened for us to explore? Just by speculating, by admitting, there is maybe the slightest possibility that our faith might have been misplaced, we have opened up a vast new potential horizon of realistic possibilities for us to pursue, then by our own volition we have the possibility of dedicating ourselves to searching within the mechanisms of god's nature, and to discover real world solutions that will help us in realizing our greatest of all of our dreams. Our god given reason is the most powerful magic for discovering and seeing our way through the darkness of ignorance, and is the only magic that can give us deliverance from our infirmities, our pain, and give us the means of extending our lives and leading us along the journey towards realizing our ultimate dream of surviving death, surviving death in reality. But as long as we are willing to continue to have "faith" in the offerings of religious magic, we are surely forever doomed, doomed for time's eternity to what history's conclusive evidence has shown to be the result of such religious faith.

There is no law of god, which speaks against our searching by means of our god given reason to discover the secrets of god, and god's glorious universe. There was never any god that forbad humans not to partake of the fruits of the tree of knowledge. It was the religious charlatans who have written in the language of some long past and dead time, that we are forbidden the fruits of the tree of knowledge. And why should these writers of falsehood, desire that knowledge be forbidden, why indeed, because they clearly understand that knowledge always, with undeniable certainty, eventually leads to the inevitable unmasking of their religious dogmas to reveal the embarrassing absurdities within all of them. Religion's dogmas, the charlatan prophets, preachers, evangelists, and ministers staunchly claim, are their god's unchanging truths, truths that are themselves eternal, truths that were secretly delivered directly from their god to the religious preachers, ministers, evangelists, and prophets, when in fact, they are nothing more than the most unbelievable of lies, lies that have been clothed within the disguise of purported holy disclosure. They are lies formulated to keep a human flock, bowing, bearing gifts, and performing endless rituals and sacrifices as a means to hopefully save their poor fearful and oppressed souls. They are lies whose devious secret purpose is to keep and to protect an enormous personal power, some of which the religious charlatans radiate along a descending chain of command, where the simple nodes of the chain are low level religious lackeys, priest, evangelists, ministers, and preachers, who are responsible to maintain both obedience to the unholy system of faith supreme, and to levee and collect from the believers an offering to their god. Although all material offerings are foreign to god, the treasures collected in their god's behalf never quite reach their god's heavenly holy throne; they are instead diverted into the temple's treasuries from where the treasures support the continuation of this system of the endless reaping of alms, which are used to prop up the religious power structure, the structure that is the sole benefactor of the whole unholy system. And the faithful believers in these so-called religious institutions, willingly deliver up to those who wear the unholy costumes of power, whatever few things of value they can be convinced to sacrifice as their offering to the religion's god. And their invisible god has never shown any great substance of good character for which he deserves any rewards whatsoever. Their god has cruelly cursed many of his innocent believers with blindness, deafness, crippled their bodies, and caused many of his believers to be racked with unbearable pain and other inhuman sufferings. How could any rational individual be convinced that this invisible uncaring god deserved even a passing notice from the peoples he has cursed with every kind of resident malady of hell? Even the common people are more caring of their own kind than is their invisible god, for they, the common people, feel deep sympathy for those of their kind who are saddled with unforgiving maladies, and the people do their very best at trying to heal and to reduce every suffering of the people who have unjustly been stricken. The common people are the ones who bravely attempt to rescue their kind from the savage painful torments of their god's hand made hells on Earth.

BRIBERY AND SACRIFICE

All religions claim they are about having faith in the gospel truth of some self named holy doctrines, which they profess were given directly to them by their god, or gods, or by some divine intermediary of their god, but the historically proven reality of their faith, is that their only real verifiable faith, is in their unshakeable faith in the ever-continuing ultimate power of the god of bribery.

It has been one of the general and most important beliefs of all religions, independent of their time in history, that their god or gods can be persuaded, nudged, enticed, lured, or seduced into yielding up special earthly favors for the enticers, if the god or gods are given certain earthly treasures as a proper offering, as a proper bribe for obtaining their favors. And in this light we see those earliest briberies, sacrifices, made to the most ancient gods, were sacrifices of what was looked upon as the greatest earthly treasure of all treasures, life's blood and life itself. The number of lives of humans and of other creature's which have been sacrificed to known and unknown gods as a direct form of holy bribery is a number whose ugly size is suspected, but is still hidden in the darkest hells of religion's past.

Their eventually came a time of increased personal enlightenment within the general population, and so religions were unable to offer up human sacrifices to their god or gods, simply because the general population would no longer sit idly by and allow such sacrifices to take place. Religions being ever able to squirm nearly without notice from one practice of doctrine to some compromise which has been forced upon them by some overwhelming public opinion, needed some replacement offering to take the place of real blood and real lives, and so they have been ever engaged in shifting their form of bribery to their god, until finally it has come to nest upon, objects of known physical value, namely money, precious metals, gems, real property, and other commonly acceptable treasures of the Earth. And in the most tenuous cases the bribery of the god or gods has come down to a verbal offering, a verbal bribery, which is made in prayer, where it is stated to the god, if you do this for me, then I promise I will be your faithful servant. And so bribery of god in one form or another is the prime method prescribed for interacting with divine beings. Of course we need to note that earthly treasures offered as bribery to the god are in fact scooped up by the religious leaders, who claim they are the intermediaries for god and will take good personal care of the sacrificial offerings, the bribes.

All ancient and modern religions genuflect at the unholy shrines of bribery, and by using this means they sustain their earthly power base, by stealing the treasures meant as a bribe to god.

THE POWER OF PRAYER

Religious leaders tell their followers their god listens to their concerns, and their god knows of all that exists, that their god sees every single sparrow that falls to Earth. Religious leaders promise that their god will answer their people's prayers of need. We as careful and understanding observers, of these proposed divine interactions between god and the people, must ask a few seemingly obvious questions. If it is true that their god listens and answers prayers, then why are there poor people? Why are there those who are homeless and hungry? Why are there millions of men, women, and children who are starving to death before their god's eyes? If their god answers their prayers, then why are there persons who are physically and/or mentally crippled? Why are some of god's children totally blind, physically and mentally? Why are some persons born without hands, arms, or legs? If their god really answers prayers, then why are there the millions upon millions who daily suffer from excruciating pain and the most horrible of diseases? If their god answers prayers, then why do floods come and indiscriminately destroy the people's homes and families without due diligence of purpose? And after the floods have passed we see and hear some of those surviving flood victims giving thanks to that same god, who must have been sleeping before and during the floods, we hear the survivors giving thanks to their god that the flood was not a worse disaster, and thanks for sparing what few things had escaped the floods disaster.

If their god answers prayers, then was their god off shopping in some distant galactic mall, when their god's people were diligently and desperately praying to be saved from the Nazi's machinery of death, which was functioning both day and night, there in god's full view, at committing the mass murders of untold numbers of helpless and innocent men, women, and children, whose prayers to their god pleaded in desperation for their god to come to their aid?

Where was this god of institutionalized religions, the one who answers prayers, when the ignorant and savage priests beat to death, strangled, then cut the throat and hacked at the body of the handsome youth who had just entered his first year of sexual maturity; then in conclusion to their obscene savage and brutal ritual of sacrifice to a now unknown god or gods, they threw what remained of the once beautiful but now lifeless youth's body into the murky dark waters of an ancient bog, where it was finally to be discovered centuries later in our modern time, and where it now bears its physical testimony to the darkest blood thirsty philosophies of ancient religions and the so-called sacrificial demands of their god or gods.

Where was this god of religions, who answers prayers, when the young girl child has her throat slit by the priests of the god, and those sick minded priests then drag the girl's struggling tender and beautiful young body through a lake's waters as the child gasps her last breaths and her sacred blood streams from her tender young neck into an uncaring lake's dark waters as a sacrifice to an even more uncaring unsympathetic God of Rain?

Where was this god who answers prayers, when Mother Nature, throughout all of history, in blind and powerful fits of undefined anger has destroyed without discrimination the temples and sanctuaries dedicated by a people devoted to the god or gods of their time, and nature's violence destroyed them without preference to what particular sect they belonged. These dedicated temples and shines of god are smashed by floods, crumbled by earthquakes, sucked and blown into pieces by nature's forces, while the inattentive god in residence, sleeps.

Where was this god who answers prayers when the invisible poisons, bacteria, and viruses of history's recorded monsters of plague, mercilessly tortured ignorant and innocent men, women, and children, while they pleaded for mercy and rescue from the invisible ghost of diseases, but instead of rescue, they were cut down with pain and suffering until they surrendered to death as the only realistic hope of relief. And this god who answers prays, where to be found was this god, in some distant corner of the universe, enjoying a barbeque?

If we are actually to believe that this god of the established religions listens to and answers prayers, then we must be blind to the burden of over whelming evidence, which is visibly in abundance throughout this world; we surely must reasonably admit that if this god is actually answering prayers, then this god hasn't been doing a very satisfactory job of it, everywhere is to be seen the massive evidence of this god's wanton neglect. It is quite clear that if we, without this institutionalized god, took due notice of what was around us then we certainly could do a much better job of helping those of our kind who sincerely need help. It's time we took notice and lay the responsibility to assist our brothers and sisters at our own doorstep, where there is at least some meager change for finding answers.

The unrecognized truth of the myth of the power of prayers is to be seen daily in how the common people of any civilized country react to providing for their worldly needs. When the people are with some serious malady, they go not to the religious temples to pray to their god or gods for relief from their suffering, but they go instead to the place where their "real faith" lies, they go to their medical doctors and to the hospitals which offer them some genuine hope of relief from their suffering. We should understand from this that your "Faith" is not where you willingly mouth it to be, but it is where, by your own actions, you have proven it to be. Most people are more than willing to wave the banners that proclaim they are faithful believers in the doctrines of the religious herds, but when we are considerate enough to observe how people actually go about the living of their lives, we can then see the truth of their beliefs independent of what they proclaim.

Teeter-totter minded philosophers say the disparity between the observable facts of life and what the proclaimers of religious doctrines presents us with is a difficult conundrum, where the truth of the matter lies within indefinable philosophical boundaries. This is utter nonsense, perpetrated by those who are too timid and too weak to step-down intellectually hard on religion's tired and ancient doctrinal feet. This timidity of course is because attached to those ancient time-worn religious feet, up-under their costumes of power, lies real power, earthly power, fear inducing power, dangerous power that the wearer's of the religious costumes have many times ruthlessly demonstrated throughout history as the only means by which they can both humble and silence their opponents, silence any and all who might dare to speak the truth of what is actually there for all to see. And as to any philosophical disparity between reality and religious doctrines, religious leaders propose these are all just a tests of the believer's faith, a test of their courage and willingness to survive and to still honor and worship their god, their proven uncaring god. It seems more likely to be a test of just how ignorant, blind, and brainwashed these foolish true believers can demonstrate that they are, even when faced with true and obvious facts.

Yes, certainly prayers are many times answered, particularly when the prayer is directed to someone who is capable of answering it.

THE NATURE OF RITUAL

It is the situation that when people, whose mentality is not critically ana-
lytic, accomplish for the first time any very complicated task, by means of
trial and error, they are never completely sure, which steps or actions
within the total steps or actions of the task were the absolutely necessary
and essential elements or actions required to accomplish the task. So as a
means to be certain that they can again successfully complete the task,
they include every element or action that they recall as being a part of the
first time the task was completed. And those elements or actions that we,
as outside observers can see as being totally without merit and irrelevant
to again successfully completing the task, these elements or actions,
which are of no realistic merit, become the ritual part of the procedure to
accomplish the task. Such ritualistic elements have, in societies where science is essentially an unknown art, become major elements in many of
the daily functioning's of people within these societies, and the people are
fearful that if the ritualistic parts are not included, then some sever
unwanted and possible evil consequence will come upon them, their
family, their village, or tribe. And so in such environments, ritual is in residence in almost all events of human endeavor. And ritual, which has no
substance relatable to real things, gives a potent birth to more-and-more
unfounded superstitions, and yet ever more rituals to supposedly protect

the people from what does not in fact exist, and whose tentacles of ignorant fear spread into most every aspect of the people's lives, who must live within these more primitive societies.

There are other natural sources of ritual. In many creatures of the animal kingdom extraordinary and elaborate rituals are sometimes performed as an important instinctive part of selecting a sexual mating partner. These instinctive rituals are passed forward through the ages of time as coding within the creature's genes.

The human creature being of a somewhat creative nature designs the structures of ritual to fit whatever they feel are their needs. And so within religious ceremonies are embedded the constructed rituals, devised by each different particular group, rituals that are meant to add a mystical theatric to what would otherwise be dull and colorless religious exhibitions. These devised rituals are sometimes quite impressive; in the best performances the rituals combine the elements of elaborate costumes, motion, smoke and mirrors, chanting, music, theatrical lighting, and glorified fixed or moving images. All is meant to inspire in the audience of viewers an emotionally stimulating awe and respect for some unseen mystical power. These performances have over the centuries been refined and rehearsed to the point that they are performed by the priestly cast as a flawless production, which has become like a second nature to them and their viewing audience.

Societies have established horrible institutions where day-in and day-out rituals are endlessly practiced, and not the slightest variation is allowed by the ritual's captive participants. We have named these institutionalized places of extreme ritual practices, "Prison." Our society's representatives of the people's will, have slowly built up an ever-expanding vast empire of prisons along with a huge army of persons, whose primary purpose is to endlessly snatch up and funnel people from a somewhat free society, and feed them through the mechanisms of a so-called system of justice, from where they are finally deposited in some prison, where their lives become completely ritualized with the most mundane repetitions of any rituals ever conceived. From these institutions of extreme ritual practices, society wins nothing of human merit and instead, these institutions systematically cultivate within their captive humanity a genuine loathing of the people and the society which imprisoned them. The prison institutions will finally return most of its imprisoned humanity back into our somewhat free society, but they will be returned with more hate and a greater practical knowledge for committing crimes against the innocent people of society than they had before they entered the ritualized system. Many, even most, of those within today's prison, should have never been placed there, they should have instead been placed into a completely different kind of institution, whose fundamental rituals are not of those of extreme restrictions, but are for genuinely offering the individual opportunities for self improvement, and it is only by this means that society has the best chance in the future of being free of worry from these once captive individuals. We, as a society, need to free our thinking from the old ways of thinking about those who are not, or ever where, a serious violent threat to us, and to offer them justice which can be seen as proportional to the supposed crime. Justice, as delivered by the archaic ritualized system we now use is clearly, without even the slightest doubt, totally out of proper proportion to the real nature of nearly any and every so-called crime, and justice within our societies has become a monster that should be fearful to every citizen.

GOD OF NOTHINGNESS

Nothing is my strength.
You cannot find me, for I am not.
My footsteps make no sound.
The past is my sanctuary.
The future is my prey.

Near to the heart of humankind sits, God, on a jeweled throne of gold. And God wears, garments, whose threads are of the best substance, bought and paid for, by labors, whose driving force, was desperate hope of escape. And God wears, gloves of finest silk, and rings of gold and gems, which bear no signs of toil, gifts, paid for, by simple folk who work the soil. And God's throne is surrounded by the beauties of art, piled, hung, and vaulted overhead, the price paid by the desperate, who wished, not to be dead. And whose form of utter emptiness, is only finally discovered, in that hour of our ultimate need, when we are inevitably deserted, and our cries of pleadings for mercy, echo through the dead jewels and other beauties of the camouflage, to the vacant and empty nothing, at the very heart of the shrine.

When allowed to act solely in its own self-interest, any religion will begin working to ban those few wonderful things that give us some little bit of pleasure in our lives. At first, they only work at banning some of those things that are obvious and understandable major pleasures for us.

Religion, given a free reign, will staunchly work at banning, one after another, each and every joy-giving act, until they finally have us in the joyless state known as religious obedience. Why should any and every religion be so interested in taking joy from our lives? Why indeed? It is simply because what they have to offer us within their so-called "house of the lord" is so boring, so mundane, so sleep inducing, that most persons who still respect their intellectual dignity stay as far away as possible from any religious services. And so who is it that attends these never ending overly repeated flamboyant rituals, wherein are repeated over-and-over again the same old unbelievable and illogical stories, which their blind preachers have been preaching for more than two thousand years. Who is it that comes forth from their dwellings and daily or weekly makes their way to the variously named temples of worship? Who indeed attends as the audience of these soporific offerings? Who?—The numb of mind, the ever following sheep, those lost beings who are unable to understand on their own any purpose of life, those desperate to be saved from unidentified ghosts, those who bear a contagious poisoned mind, those who dress as a spectacle of their success, and other persons who see it all as a kind of neighborhood social club, those who desire to somehow be seen by others as holy and near to god, and to be seen as a kind of special nobility which they believe is above nonbelievers, and all of those others, who out of fear are afraid to boycott the religious herd. The followers, the audience, comes as willing dupes to eternally hear what they have already heard before, to be continually brainwashed beyond any hopeful chance of seeing the world around them differently, than that world whose meaning has already been interpreted for them by some religious dogma. There are just two kinds of people who willingly grace the halls and temples of religion, those who know better than to believe in the doctrines and have their own hidden motives, and then there are those who truly do not know any better than to believe the false religious doctrines.

We can begin to understand that religions are privately afraid, if we have any source of joy in our lives, we will choose that source of joy over attending their ever repeating, never ending, dull, dull ceremonies, and their stories which all can see are bold faced lies, all performed within their so-called "houses of the lord." The evidence is there to behold by anyone who cares to see it. Religions when free to work their will unhindered, use every means to destroy joy and pleasures. Given the free opportunity religions, have and will ban music, song, and dance, not allowing it to be seen or performed. Religions have and will ban the artist and the art of painting, ban the sculptor and the sculptings, ban books that tell a different story from that of their liking, ban thinkers who think thoughts that reach beyond their simple minded closed religious philosophies, ban medicine from searching into areas not explicitly condoned within religion's unholy holy books. We have seen that in some countries religions has even banned the flying of kites. The list of what is or might be banned by over zealous religious persons is a list without any logical or reasonable ending. It seems certain that if they had the power to do it, the religious powers would ban the smiles and laughter from our faces, and thereby leave us completely without any expressions of joy and pleasure.

CREATURES OF
CREATION

Nature is the relentless changer, whose moods wane and flux with mercy to none, and who makes for each life-form some ever-greater test that sorts and sifts and determines, which kind will be buried by time, or, which will live to see tomorrow's new sunrise. During the billions of years of evolution's flux, Mother Nature herself has cried no tears for those who were pushed aside, she has buried them without ceremony or thought, her laws are invincible and final, and she accepts no prayers to take back any of her moves in the game of evolution, which all of living creation is solemnly obliged to play with her.

Nature's laws tromp the way and even she must obey as they drum out tomorrow's new song. From the melody of mists veiling the past where small things wiggle and swim, from the beat of thunder and fire over the plains where great beasts rage, from the rhythms of fur, warmth, and sweet milk for suckling, she looks back now, through our eyes, her eyes, to see where she has wandered, blind, and crippled, while always protecting her hidden dream of sight. And now a tear, for some things ended, flows hot down her fleshy cheek of creation.

Now Mother Nature is manifested in our bodies, and we, as she, stands on the shoulders of the beast that was her blind and crippled past. She can now know, with this first spring of real understanding, things that in her long gestation were only felt as unidentifiable occurrences within the nightmare of time endlessly rushing onward to some distant future, some hidden destiny's conclusion. She can, through our eyes, begin to dimly see the perpetual melody of life dancing in the first particles of her most distant, distant past.

We seeing and falsely believing that we understand, see ourselves, our kind, as wise as any creature that has ever been, as a creature of great compassion and one that contains the holy substance of intellect. We see ourselves, our kind, as scientists, artist, lovers, creators, dreamers, and partial to all good things of character and of action. But, most of the other creatures of nature see us with the eyes of their instinctive nature, and they see us as the most dangerous monster within all of creation. They see us as the uncaring creature that unjustly occupies the territories of their natural ownership. They see us as a monster that will wantonly slaughter them without reason or the slightest provocation. They see us as the monster that eats their young as a delicate appetizer before gorging upon mounds of scared flesh. They know us as the creature that without even the slightest causative reason will suddenly destroy anything within reach. Who then knows the truth of what we are and how nature sees our kind, and whose judgment in the end will weight which facts or fantasies of our being, are to be of the heaviest weight, those of our desires, of our blind beliefs, of our undeniable history, or those other instinctive eyes of our neighboring creatures who have watched us from their special and unique perspective. And the creature that we truly are, is a mix of all these perceptions, and none of them can be denied. And to be the sum of all good and bad is not a banner that we should too proudly wave about, but is one that needs some serious correcting.

Near to the heart of humankind sits, on a great throne of sticks and grasses, a creature who sees itself above all other classes. A creature that can move faster than all, and can fly through the air, and hardly ever fall; can swim all seas without even a second breath, can even swim under them, defying death. A creature that makes its own music for singing and dance, a creature so cleaver to create its own games of chance. A creature with instruments that can look to the stars. A creature with the luxury of having its own cars. The truth of this matter must clearly be shown. This creature stands by itself not alone; it stands on the shoulders of all that came before, each mold, each grass, each crawler, and more, each swimmer, each flyer, gave some of their kind, to make this creature see things so blind. It believes that it is the ultimate top of all, but it's really a bit of all the rest, which allows it to stand so tall.

SEX

Just how do most religions approach sex? They ban certain kinds of acts, from the multitude of sexual acts that can bring us great pleasure, along with the accompanying physical and mental bonding which is a primary part of the mystic ritual of sex, and given enough time, they will soon enough, have some kind of religious taboo attached to each of the most stimulating acts for obtaining sexual satisfaction. When religion is allowed, it will leave us with only one religiously acceptable sexual act, and that of course bears the name of its simple minded founders, "The Missionary Position." It would seem that only god knows, as is commonly said, how many different possibilities there are for having stimulating joyful sex, but if you let religion, or a government influenced by religion, to condemn on any grounds one of the sexual possibilities, then you are opening up the door for a religion to next decide that maybe your way of enjoying sex is to become the next unholy no—no, and then you will be the one to be persecuted, not by god, but by an ignorant arrogant and nearly logically blind religious society. Some religions now see even the most basic and fundamental sex needed for the reproduction of our kind as, a dirty necessity, which our bodies must perform to the disgust of our observant holy spirit.

There can be little doubt that within the animal kingdom, the nature of each creature's sex and sexuality are determined by factors of heredity. But whereas both the physical and mental characteristics relating to an individual's sexuality are determined by heredity, the nature of the physical and mental aspects of an individual's sexuality are not necessarily the same.

The instincts involved in sexual attraction are highly driven by visual cues, which tell something about the overall condition of the body and about some very specific features of the body. The appearance of the hips, waist, buttock and breast are very important instinctive sexual stimulators. The image of a face being symmetrical has a great importance in determining sexual desirability. When the facial image is symmetrical it is seen as beautiful. It has been suggested that regular symmetry of the face and head is an indication that the individual's head and what is inside of the head is genetically OK.

In general, when one is visually determining the sexual desirability of some potential partner, there always takes place a quick visual scanning of the potential partner's overall body. If the body looks generally symmetrical, it is a powerful indication that it was derived from a good and complete set of inheritable genetic instructions. Since the sexual instinct is truly older than the hills, "instinctive sexual desirability," as rated by nature's sexual instinct, is all about a symmetric and strong muscular or plump physical body, which is what Mother Nature rates as "Prime Meat" in her rules concerning what it takes for simply surviving in a vicious world. Truthfully in the world of instinctive sexual desirability, there is no natural sexual attraction for the intellectual abilities of a potential mate. Be cognizant that here we are talking about sex and sexual desire, and the instincts, which drive two sexual partners together to have sex. These sexual instincts have nothing whatsoever to say about choosing a partner for any kind of long lasting compatible and stable relationship, a relationship where the partner's intellectual characteristics and not their physical characteristics are the primary

long term stabilizing elements. The "Sexual Instincts" are all about get-
ting down to having sex, and nothing else. In our present societies, we
allow the sexual instincts to overcome our intellect, and let them drag
us into marriages, which were primarily based on our powerful instinctive sexual attractions, this gives the marriage little chance of happily
surviving the winds of time. Both men and woman look for the physical
determinative sexual indicators within each other. If all of the correct
physical parts are signaling sexual attraction, but some body movement
tells a negative story, or there is discovered some physical damage, or
there is some appearance of sickness, or some weakness, then all of the
sense of sexual attraction can be immediately canceled.

Since the sexual instincts are one of the most powerful of all our
instincts, and since they are very much about establishing an unusually
strong attraction towards the observable physical characteristic of a
potential mate, we should guess that the sexual attraction is also
affected by the potential mate's display of their body language. Consider
the very strong emotional bonds that most all children establish with
their parents, independent of whether the parents of the child are, or
are not, their biological parents. We must suspect, as is sometimes said,
that when choosing a mate, a male looks to find a mate that in some
ways resembles his mother, and a female looks to find a mate that in
some ways resembles their father, let's call this phenomenon the
"Father-Mother-Attraction Axiom". As concerns two mated persons, we
can, by simply observing their dominant physical characteristics, often
see that this Father-Mother-Attraction Axiom seems quite often to be
true. But if we could also see the common body language relationships
that might exist between the mated persons and their parents, we might
again discover, that in this way, the Father-Mother-Attraction Axiom
has again been validated. We can never be entirely sure, as to what physical and body language characteristics of a parent, are those most
strongly and indelibly written into a child's memory, and are for the
child, the primary identifying factors that represent their parents. But,

when we are considering the mother's and father's characteristics that make up the bonding image which is indelibly written into a child's mind, the image is necessarily one which was formed very early in the child's lifetime. So it is this earliest image of their parents that the grown child looks to find within their potential mate. If we could know these factors, I'm sure we would then be able to more clearly see that the Father-Mother-Attraction Axiom is a major final factor in the choosing of a mate. It is, as if Mother Nature is saying, "This combination worked well before, so let's try it again."

It is sadly true, within most societies throughout the world that they attempt to forcefully warp sexual attraction into social and legally binding contracts of marriage. In a more distant time of our past, such binding contracts where about nurturing and protecting the offspring, which in those days would be the inevitable result of most sexual relationships. Today, there are those persons aboard their hypocritical battleships, who seem to be ignorant of the powers of Mother Nature's sexual instincts, and they bombard society with slogans about sexual abstinence, just as if once the cork is coming out of the bottle of champagne it can be indefinitely stopped at the bottle's lip.

Our societies are so plagued with religion's multitudes of sexual no-nos that the natural sexual instincts have been so warped, contorted, and forcefully transmuted, that our peoples are totally confused about the real meanings of romance, sex, love, and long term personal relationships. Sex should never be used as the sole driving force behind marriage, or for any other long-term personal bonding.

A very strange abnormal situation exists in our so-called modern world. We live in a world were the religious authorities and their conditioned puppets of power, a long with their brain washed public supporters are absolutely rabid in every respect about any sexual relationships, which are not about producing children. These people are also nearly thrown in a spastic frenzy, should they discover that a child has seen or heard of any kind of material of a sexual nature. Have any of these self-proclaimed sexual control police ever taken a good look at the natural world of the other animals. You can clearly see within the natural world that the Great Creator God has displayed there for all to view every kind of sexual behavior that could possibly be imagined, and there is no natural censoring curtain that can be drawn over what takes place there, the real Great Creator God sees absolutely nothing there, which requires being either censored or in anyway hidden from anyone.

The days are hopefully long gone when every sexual encounter necessarily produces a child. If society is to ever be truly psychologically healthy, then sex must have its open place in societies, and hopefully become as natural a pleasure as is any of the other of nature's wonderful sensual pleasures. Persons living within a mentally healthy society should have a place of safety, where they can visit and share a sexual experience based on mutually acceptable terms of the sexual participants. For any society to condemn and to discourage sexual activities between sexually mature individuals inevitably leads to the opening of a Pandora's box from where emerges upon society the most horrible and unbelievable of sex crimes; all stemming from repressed sexual desires which are then satisfied, by sexually tormented individuals, upon unwilling partners. And these kinds of forced sex acts, perpetrated upon unwilling partners, are so prevalent within today's societies that they should stand as a logical condemnation of the unnatural sexual taboos, which are their primal cause and brought them into existence. Sexual relationships that do not produce children should not have any place on anyone's philosophical radar screen.

Mother Nature's prime interest in heterosexual relationships is her concern to get the female's egg or eggs fertilized at any cost. In Mother Nature's relentless drive to get the egg fertilized, she was forced into selecting a system of unequal desires and unequal sexual performance between the two sexual components, male and female. Natural selection has necessarily selected for males who are able to perform the sexual act and to quickly have an ejaculation with its accompanying satisfying orgasm as the signature that their sexual function has been fulfilled. On the other hand, natural selection has necessarily selected for those females who were much slower than males in being able to obtain sexual satisfaction during the time of sexual intercourse, and also in selecting for females who are unable to ever have a sexual orgasm during the time of normal sexual intercourse. There are some women who will freely admit that it is difficult or impossible for them to have an orgasm during sexual intercourse, but it is sure, if the truth were known, that many, many more women than now admit to this situation, would also have to admit to it.

The seemingly unfair difference in the time it takes for males and females to reach a state of sexual satisfaction during sexual intercourse is a prime contributor to the survival of our kind, and to the survival of the other creatures of nature who sexually reproduce.

These seemingly unfair natural differences are absolutely necessary as a means of guaranteeing the female's egg has the best chance of being fertilized, because if the female was naturally able to reach a satisfying orgasm during sexual intercourse before the male experienced an orgasm, she would likely push the male away as soon as she had been satisfied, and this situation would not allow her egg to become fertilized. By Mother Nature selecting for the disparity in the time it takes the male and female partners to gain some sexual satisfaction, nature has chosen a method that gives the best possibility for the female's egg to become fertilized during sexual intercourse. Sadly for the females of the modern world, we find that because of nature's natural selection, that most females are unable to have a sexual orgasm during the time it takes for a male to perform his part of sexual intercourse and to reach his satisfying sexual climax. There are many females who are unable to have a sexual orgasm by any means. Therefore in modern times, where the production of children is most often of a secondary concern in sex, and where mutual joyful pleasure is the primary concern, then for both the male and female partners to have a mutually satisfying sexual encounter, it should be considered that sexual means, other than just sexual intercourse, might offer a better possibility for realizing some kind of mutual sexual satisfaction. Male partners need to be educated that sexual intercourse might be a curse for their female partners in not being able to achieve sexual satisfaction, and that other methods might prove to be more satisfying for both partners.

It's a cruel trick that Mother Nature has laid upon the females, but its results have been very successful for each species.

No one can say with absolute certainty that any women can actually have an orgasm in a like manner as is had by males. It seems that the physical mechanisms necessary to produce an orgasm are simply missing in a women's anatomy. In our present time where females are struggling for their equal place in all aspects within a world that has previously been dominated by males, it was only natural that females should lay claim to their equality in the previously exclusive world of a male's sexual satisfaction through male orgasm. Many women of today are unwilling to bow down to any proclaimed differences between the two sexes. And so the idea of a female orgasm equal in every way to that had by males soon took root and gained in popularity and even spread to the so-called sex specialists of the medical community. It is nearly unthinkable that anyone should now days question the truth of the sexual equality of the female orgasm, which is professed as a reality. We might see how ridiculous is this demand that all things between the two sexes must be equal, consider if males, not wanting to seem lesser in any respect than females, started claiming that they are in fact equal to women in every respect, and they are fully capable of having babies, but they are doing it secretly, off and away from were the truth of the matter can be seen. Surely the males are here faking it, but then?

If we would like some supporting evidence to better decide about this female orgasm controversy, we might find it in other members of creation, particularly among those creatures that do not have a complex spoken language with which they can say what is true, verses what they physically demonstrate is true. Let's look at the female mammals and discern if they do, or do not, have sexual orgasms during their sexual intercourse. We can look to the mammals other than our kind and see what their natural actions can tell us in truth about this matter. The other mammals cannot by means of spoken language lie to us about their sexual activities. We can see the truth of this matter in how the females behave within a sexually active group in their natural environment. We see the females, in a sense, are only waving their asses in the air, when they are in heat and are in need of having their egg or eggs fertilized. And when they are not in heat, they are uninterested in any sexual activity with any male. We should believe that if female mammals had a sexual orgasm during sexual intercourse, as male mammals do, then females would also be very interest in having sex regularly and frequently even when they are not in heat, as males are always interested in sex. Males, knowing in reality the pleasure of the sexual orgasm, are very much interested in experiencing another orgasm at nearly any and every opportunity.

It can't be denied that women can experience some kind of emotional reaction to some sexual stimulation other than at those times she is in heat. And it would seem that these emotional reactions can be lasting and satisfying, but they are not the equivalent of a male's orgasm. In this respect some women say that they can have multitudes of orgasms during sexual intercourse, but if these purported orgasms were in any way equivalent to the orgasm that males experience, then it is sure that such women would require intensive long term hospital care as a means of recovering from the series of powerful impacts to their emotional psyche. If a male experienced multitudes of orgasms during sexual intercourse, he would be physically unable to move, and would need to be confined to his bed until he was able to emotionally recover from such an overpowering physical and emotional experience. So there are clearly some disparities between what some women report about their orgasms, and what is physiologically believable, and also what is believable as is evidenced within other female mammals, who seem to go about sex as a kind of rather boring necessity and not as any great thing of sensual pleasure.

I hope you are now wondering, if most women, and possibly all women, are not having a sexual orgasm during sexual intercourse, in the same manner that males can physically and mentally experience an orgasm, then what is it that so powerfully attracts women into strongly desiring and engaging in sexual acts. The truth of this matter is that the forces of sexual desire are not in the first instance about obtaining an orgasm. Those first demanding and all powerful forces of attraction, which drive our kind into first desiring close intimate physical contact with an other, and which very soon can lead to the sexual act, are nature's instinctive desire, as it is sometimes said, "To Have" the person of our desire. This powerful drive **to have** the person of our instinctive desire is common in initializing the sexual act for both women and men. This part of the sexual instincts, **to have,** is much about driving us into a situation that results in providing proof of our mutual acceptance of each other. The fact that the inevitable result of this situation, our powerful desire **to have** another person in our physical possession, and which eventually can lead to sexual intercourse or some other sexual act that results in an orgasm is a mere secondary consequence of the initial driving force. This, **"desire to have,"** is a part of the sexual instincts that is the ethereal substance of the physical and mental aspects of desire, romance, love, and friendships. Real love is actually about this initial driving force of the sexual instincts, the desire to have, to be near to, to become a spiritual part of another person. Many persons, both men and women, are driven by this desire to have an other person, and they are sometimes quite willing and driven by strong desires to satisfy another person, sexually, or other wise, without any concern for themselves finding any physical sexual satisfaction in the experience, but they instead find a satisfaction of equal merit in the fulfilling of their desire "To Have." This is all just a bit difficult to explain in exacting terms simply because it is all about feelings, which are not readily definable with words. But, this part of the sexual instincts, **"the drive to have,"** gives us the desire for physical contact, to be in the neighborhood of those we desire, to dream and think of those who we desire. This "To Have" part of the sexual instincts is common to most of the more advanced creatures of nature and is surely what can draw females temporarily into close contact with males, who are interested in pursuing more that just closeness. It is clear that in many creatures during the time the female is in estrus, their **"to have,"** desires are so heightened, they use every means at advertising their desires to be both accommodating and close, and to be **"had."** But this is not directly about their desire to satisfy something sexual, it is merely Mother Nature's trap that makes a sexual relationship possible and probable. We see within the human population some women and men are so driven by the need **to have,** that they are unable to control their desire. It must be a common situation for those persons in society who become the stalkers of others.

Each of us is born with a predetermined sexual preference, which certainly is determined by hereditary factors. It does not take much investigation to understand that individuals, from their earliest years, have strong feelings concerning the direction of their sexual orientation. They did not have to be schooled to know it. They did not have to be brainwashed to know it. Their sexual orientation was upon them naturally from the time of their earliest feelings for others within their species. It is quite clear from listening to many individual testimonies that whatever a person's sexual orientation might be, that it was there as a natural condition of their being, and that it remains constantly the same and unchanged throughout their lifetime as does any inherited trait.

When we consider sexual preference for persons of the same sex, we come upon some rather unusual circumstances. If we are thoughtful, we are forced to wonder about the genetic nature of this instinct. It would seem highly unusual if its source was genetic in nature, since in present society it is commonly believed that members of this group do not reproduce themselves. It is an undeniable fact of nature that if a kind does not reproduce itself, then eventually its kind dies and becomes extinct. Also, you simply do not get elephants by breading rabbits. If in fact, you should like to believe that this trait, this instinct, is not inherited, then you are faced with a miracle in nature that is equivalent to a virgin birth.

Careful consideration might leads us to believe, that because of the extreme pressures of the "Herd," many in this group are socially forced into acting against their real sexual preference for their same sex. And because of the nearly unbearable pressures from the dominant social herds, they feel forced into a heterosexual marriage, where they also feel obligated to produce children. In our society to have children is generally considered as the triumphal and undeniable proof of the parent's heterosexuality. By means of an essentially herd forced marriage, and its resulting children the genes for this sexual instinct are passed on to some of their offspring. This seems the most reasonable and understandable way for this particular sexual instinctive trait to have survived throughout all of recorded time.

It would seem the most logical assumption, that sexual preference is instinctive in essentially all cases.

This then must lead us to some further unusual speculations. Within the general population estimates for the percentages of the population that profess to a sexual preference for the same sex is in a low percentage range of around five to ten percent. I believe that based on the assumption that this instinct is most likely an inherited instinct, we have to consider that it exists in a much larger percentage of the population. Just considering the proportions of a normal bell curve, and that many within this sexual preference group are forced by society's herd pressures to disavow their natural sexual preference instinct, then we can be very suspicious of the usually reported numbers. It is more likely true,

that somewhere near 5% are in manner, as this whole group is characterized, and it is somewhat easy, by merely observing their body language, to identify those members of the group. Just keeping in mind the
normal bell curve as applied to this group, but speaking of percentages
as applied to the overall general population, it is reasonable to believe
that there is another five percent, who are members of this group, but
are mannered like alpha males or alpha females, and they simply exist in
society totally unsuspected of their real sexual preference. We are still
left to consider those persons represented at the middle of the curve. At
the middle of the curve some ten to fifteen percent must lie somewhere
between the two extremes at the ends of the curve, and they necessarily
must have discernable characteristics that are a moderation of those
more extreme characteristics represented at the two ends of the curve.
Those in the middle of the curve surely have traits that are relatively
indiscernible from fully heterosexual individuals. We should also keep
in mind that those in the middle of the curve have characteristics and
inclinations that span between homosexuality and heterosexuality. We
might reasonably suppose that if the general population was not inhibited by the unnatural condemnations of the herd, that as many as fifty
percent of the population might be willing to freely express, and happily engage in bisexual behavior, which they do not see as an unnatural
behavior. Within the population, of the middle and upper curve percentages, most persons who are part of this group are surely married
persons and most of them surely have children, a fact that might be
reflected in-part by the high divorce rate and the serious unhappiness
among those who stay married, either because of duty to their children
or for other less noble reasons, such as their financial situation. Many of
those who stay married certainly have a life with some happiness, but it
must be certain, because of the most powerful nature of this sexual
instinctive drive, they must have a chronic feeling of dissatisfaction with
their situation, and of their life being in some way unfulfilled. Based on
these considerations we might be suspicious of the reasons for the high

rate of suicide among teenagers. It is sad to note that the teenage suicide rate appears to be the highest in those areas of the nation where religious influence is most dominant, and where religious intolerance against this group is the strongest. Within the over-all population of those whose sexual orientation is directed towards their same sex, there are those persons who feel driven to hide their true feelings simply because of the nearly overwhelming condemnation, which comes from various herds and their associations with institutionalized religions. There are therefore many homosexuals who remain hidden within society, and as a means of camouflage, they use the age-old adage that "The best defense is a powerful offense." They therefore try to hide their own instinctive sexual nature, by waging a vengeful and unforgiving war against their own kind. Sigmund Freud pointed out this very situation. Not being open about their own same sex preference, they usually hide behind some mythical righteous fortress from where they hurl their insults and condemnations against their own kind.

Any non-bigoted and serious religious scholar of the unholy holy books will tell you, that just because something has been written there, it does not mean that it is the word of any god. The unholy holy books are collections of somewhat historical writings, written by men, and as such those men had their own personal and social axes to grind. During the period of history that the unholy holy books span, any sexual act that did not result in the bearing of children had to be absolutely forbidden. Each tribe's survival was dependent on their women producing the greatest numbers of children, simply as a means of trying to balance out a nature that took them as a sacrifice to their time's gods of ignorance. In ancient times, an average mother was lucky to have just two or three of her children survive to the time of their sexual maturity. To encourage the family to "Be fruitful and multiply" and to damn any and every sexual activity that did not produce children was a tribe's, a city's, a nation's main philosophy for survival, and not just surviving, but a growth in its numbers and therefore in their world, which was absolutely dominated by religious herds, to grow in power.

Even a casual examination, of societies and their culture's throughout history, indicates conclusively that there does not exist any natural instinctive bias against homosexuality. It is clear that all biases against members of this group are perpetrated by various "Institutions of the Herds" that feel they have something special to gain for themselves by condemning members of this group. And what it is—they feel they gain—is babies—many, many, many new babies, who are destine to become the new members of their religious herd.

It is quite understandable why Mother Nature has never produced any instinctual biases against homosexuality, and it is simply because those who are male members of this group do not generally engage in the competition with the other males, for female reproductive mates, so there is no reason for the heterosexual males to be biased against them. And, dominant heterosexual males have always systematically raped those members of the group, who are physically female.

We can often see in the boldest of unequivocal terms, how some members of dominant herds are willing to demonstrate their obvious ignorance and their own hypocrisy by persecuting members of their herd who are discovered to be homosexuals. We have seen, all too often, when some soldier has been greatly honored for their exceptional positive contributions to their military organization, and then at some later date it is discovered that the same soldier is a homosexual, then instantly, the military organization withdraws their already given honors, and labels the soldier as an undesirable person and discharges them from the military organization. There are those within our military organizations who don't mind publicly displaying their irrational, illogical, and hypocritical way of thinking, it is those persons who should be publicly dishonored and discharged from their military service, and if those same persons were ever to command our beloved young soldiers in a combat situation, then pray to every god to save our soldiers from their kind of illogical thinking. The military services should, by all good logic, be pleased and overjoyed at having within their organizations, homosexuals who desire to militarily serve their country. Why? Because all homosexuals, who live within our loving, caring, forgiving, so called religious society, have by the time they are eighteen years of age, already survived eighteen years of a kind of extended "Boot Camp" that was for them, a social hell, a hell where it is physically and psychologically more difficult for an individual to survive, than to survive in any military boot camp. They survived our religious society's social boot camp of hell, which a stupid, ignorant, and intolerant falsely professed religious society has forced them to endure as just a part of their growing up.

The time may not be too far off before we might be able to identify the specific genes that govern the instinct for sexual preference. I believe it would be the gravest error, if we tried to vary the gene structure of any individual to change their same sex preference to opposite sex preference. Mother Nature has, in her own time-tested wisdom, somehow given us this instinctive same sex preference. It surely is there for a good purpose, even if we in our ignorance do not exactly understand. As a society by meddling with this instinct, we could suffer a major loss of creative talent. Our history bears witness to the greatly disproportionate high number of meaningful contributions made by individual members of this group. They have been some of the world's greatest political leaders, military leaders, philosophers, teachers, scientists, artist and athletes. It certainly seems that coupled with this instinct, is a different way of seeing and understanding the world, and because of it, society has been privileged to receive insights and other contributions from the members of this group, that others rarely find. Any society, which nourishes their community of homosexuals to flourish in safety, always wins with their honoring of diversity, a great advantage of insight and creativity, which significantly contributes to new discoveries in every field. We need to, at every opportunity, stand up against those near-sighted fools, who without logic or any good reasoning attempt to condemn members of this group, as the members of this group are one of the most valuable human resources that any nation can ever hope to have working for a better future for all.

Independent of sex and sexual preferences, the time is long over due, when societies should consider other opportunities, which can provided even stronger stabilizing social elements, than those ideas which are from the distant past and are still being forced down our throats as the necessary and only social elements that can stably bind society together. A much more powerful philosophy, which is ever-more capable of commonly binding society into a more individually satisfying and a more functional social group, is to be had by simply recognizing that persons of the same sex generally find they have more common understandings and are more emotionally suited to living with each other, than they are suited to living with their opposite sex, and they daily gain a greater satisfaction from living with their own sex, independent of whether they share sexual pleasures or not. Persons of the same sex who like each other and who get along well together, because they share common interests, usually discover that their life together becomes both emotionally comfortable and pleasant, which is something more than can be said of the situation within many marriages and many families. Society needs to change away from those stringent inflexible ideas about what cements the social fabric and yet results in so much unhappiness within the social fabric. Society needs to promote and honor personal linkings, which give the individual the best possibilities to be creatively productive and to better seek out their own happiness.

THE INDIVIDUAL

Nature has just four kinds of kisses.
The kiss of life
The kiss of hope
The kiss of despair
And the kiss of death

After eons of time and our more recent pains-taking meticulous seeking and discovering, we can now clearly see that we are sitting on a branchlet of a limb of the tree of life, which represents our divine family, our sacred holy family of Apes.

In all of nature's life, throughout all of time, in every species, in every family, in every genus, it is the individual who bears the lonesome stamp of uniqueness, and it is an individual who is inevitability and ultimately the survivor of its mother's kind. It is the genotype, the individual, whose subtle differences, like some artist gentle brush stroke, a mere blush of color, a slight bend of a line, the hint of a different texture, that takes the new higher step up on nature's subtle multifaceted staircase which leads to a new tomorrow's sunrise.

Nearly hidden in the ruckus drive of human history, not noticed by those who can only see the main over-bearing, exploding blaze of it all, is the struggle for the individual to be free. The gross show, is the ups and downs of tyrants and their empires, but amongst the never-ending theatrical clamor of history, where new tyrants in new disguises always occupy center stage, in the background of this, as a sweeter melody that refuses to be lost, is the continuous never ending struggle of the individual to be free, and this struggle although buried within the ramparts of history's onward march, is what the progress of history is secretly all about.

Historians have in many instances written history as if the great accomplishments of a particular period where directly attributable to whatever religion was dominant within the period's social structure or within a particular empire. And historians frequently praise the scientific, philosophical, artistic, and technical accomplishment as if they were a direct product of the time's religion, but these things are never the accomplishments of some religion of a period, they are each and every one of them, the accomplishments of individuals who by happenstance lived and contributed their creations within the society where they lived during that period. As evidence of this as a believable fact, those very same religions, who during one time period of their history bathed themselves in the praise of the accomplishments of the very creative individuals living within their religious doctrine's area of domination, we can now see those very same religions, and the individuals, who still live submerged within the very same religious doctrines, making no offerings of any significance at all, yet if the historian's story is to be believable, as to the contributions, then we need to ask ourselves, why is this same religious society, not still making great creative contributions in the realms of science, philosophy, the arts, and technology. The simple and understandable truth of the matter is when individualism is nourish it automatically blooms forth with creative ideas and this blooming happens not because of stagnating religious doctrines, but in spite of them. Religions are always fast at claiming the accomplishments of an individual, as if the accomplishment belong to them, and are always more than fast to shy away from any of their individual's acts that might be seen as offensive. Religions rush to willingly stumble over themselves to take credit for any good accomplishment of a member or group living within their religious domain, but they attempt to remain invisible when any of their members or groups commits some major fault. Only social philosophies that respect and nurture diversity, non-dogmatic discovery, and learning can be given any part of the historical credit for the accomplishments of individuals living within their time, and these conditions are foreign to most every religious doctrine. If we are to understand why one period of history is more creative than another, it is always because of the diversity of ideas, which flux between individuals within the society, and not for any other reason.

It is clear within human history, that although there has been a somewhat steady progress towards recognizing the value of the individual, the emphasis of major efforts has always been to subjugate the individual to the needs of the society. Society's needs are held as some cherished holy law, which consistently relegates the needs of the individual to some always-lesser place than the needs of society. Although new nations of recent history have gift wrapped in constitutional papers some declared sacred reference to the rights and freedoms of the individual, in actual practice, those same nations ignore those declarations whenever some conflict exists between the rights of the individual verses the discerned needs of the society. And so our world of today pays lip service to individual freedoms, while willingly stomping down those freedoms in the name of the higher ideal, the society. This is a sad error, whose immediate effect is to stagnate both the individual and the society, and whose eventual ultimate culmination, can lead to both the destruction of the individual and the society. It should be hoped, considering today's relatively enlightened understandings of nature and our position within the structures of nature, that at last, we can begin to understand that only by making the individual the cherished holy shrine of societies and cultures, can those societies and cultures prosper and continue to advance with both meaning and dignity. We must now, after painful eons of our worshiping the group, the tribe, the society, the religion, realize it is within the free exercise of individualism and the unique creations, which spring solely from that source, that our hopes for an ever-better future reside.

Near to the heart of humankind sits, on a tarnished and rusting throne, an image, by itself, alone. And through the depth of its meaning runs, a golden thread of hope with no end. Throughout history's long continuous dance of triumph and pain, there is one, just one thread of hope, which winds its way continuously from time's beginning to the present. Even through times not on history's written page, this tread of hope cuts its way through molds and slimes, through steaming forests, through ancestors whose words of truth were grunts and groans. It runs, this tread of hope, through all of evolution, and through ours too, where now it finds voice, which names it true. In all of history's fanfares, turmoil, defeats; blinding clouds of smoke and fiery camouflage', amidst the loud rumble of nations on the rise, hidden in the dust shrouded cries as they fall, is one, just one struggle, common to them all. It is the struggle to bow no more to dominant strength of flesh and bone, to costumes of power, to priests, or kings, or tyrants, or illogical gods. That thread of hope represents, the individual's struggle to know for themselves, what is true and right. And not to accept unchallenged, taboos lying on a sacrificial alter, which has been drawn with ancient ropes, by an army of ignorant ghostly laborers, out of the pit of the dark, dark past. That thread of hope is the individual's struggle to be free, to be themselves, to be an individual, and not to be afraid to be uniquely different.

The most significant part of the Great God of Creation is the individual, it is to god, the individual who is holy, is sacred, and is our only hope for a future salvation. Without this belief our kind with all its dynamic and grandiose schemes for survival is utterly doomed. It is not some fictional idea of a race, or a family of animals, which has given us survival within the long history of nature's evolution, but it is the individual, which by their unique differences yields up the alternatives necessary for survival in an ever-changing world.

It was not humans as a group, who discovered or invented agriculture. It was an individual. We, as a group, never-ever came upon any aspect of nature, and as a group said, look at this marvelous event of nature, we can do such and such with it, and it will better our lives. We are not a family like Donald Duck's nephews, who each one speaks a single word to make one complete sentence. We are not an animal of a natural communist persuasion. We are not and should not be an animal subject solely to democratic style, which in the strictest sense is a philosophy of anti-minority and anti-individualism. We are each alone in seeing, hearing, tasting, smelling and touching the creation, and therefore each person's understanding should always be open for expressing what they have discovered. We should set as a personal goal, that we will encourage and strive to sanctify the dignity of the individual over the cries for subjugating the individual to some faked group's fantasy that their cause always has the higher priority. The formulas for coagulating our kind into groups of types, or races, are all worthless garbage from a dying past, and to continue to worship at that shrine is surely a pathway leading to our eventual doom or an eventual hell on Earth, whichever comes first.

Any physical or definable mental characteristic which can in any way, by means of its mark, place us into some common group whose primary identifier is that mark, is sufficient to establish each of us as the member of some kind of minority group. Some few examples should establish an understanding for the bases of our case, such as: the color of one's skin, the color of the eyes, the color of the hair, a person's height, their weight, the style of the clothing they wear, the kind of music they prefer, or any other trait which could be used as a means of placing an individual into a group, where all the members of the group share that common trait. We are, each one of us, subjected by the silly rules of a flippant society, to being discriminated against because we happen to be an involuntary member of some unnatural grouping, where the common characteristic of the group is insignificant in defining the real substance, the over powering predominant substance of what and who we are as individuals. There are millions upon millions who have identifiable common traits, but not one of those common traits, not even one, have by any means of logical reasoning, any meaning which can point to who we are, and the unseen, untouchable, fluxing of our individual minds, which is what primarily makes us each uniquely and overwhelmingly different from any possible single identifying trait. We are as different individuals, substantially and primarily only what we have learned and remembered during the time we have been alive. It is the person who is identifiable as a unique individual, who has the most, and the most varied information as memories within their mind. It is the contents of our own mind that primarily determines just how unique we are, how much of an actual "Individual" we are. And it is the tolerance and nourishment that a society actually gives to help its citizens into becoming valued unique individuals, valuable to themselves and to our society, that is the true measure of its worth to us all.

As individuals we are willing to make any fight or pay any cost, if there is the chance that we might live life for a few more days, and we secretly hope that within a few more days, there might be a new chance for extending our life again for another few more days, and we secretly hope that within a few more days there might be the chance of extending our life again, and so this story repeats-and-repeats until hope is finally lost to death, the place where the dream that was us, vanishes into an unknown, unknown. We should ever be striving and working for a time when the story of hope for a few more days, never ends. But if we keep writing off our failures and shortcomings as "just the way things are," or as "one of the realities of life," then those same failures will be with us forever. Why shouldn't we want to give up to the idea of "That's the way it is, and that's the way it will always be." How more hopeful, and how more sure for finding a better future, it is to dream a better dream, and then try to make that dream come true.

More than a third of what we are as unique individuals is determined solely by what we have learned. And that third, along with some of our instincts which have been superbly enhanced, is in truth what mainly sets us apart from all of the other animals; it is not any greater physical dexterity of our hands, or our two long legs, or our erect posture that sets us so far apart from the other animals, it is what we have learned, the knowledge that we have gained determines the size of gulf between us and the other animals, and the size of the gulf that separates us from the others within the groups and herds of our own kind. So our greatest dream is for everyone to religiously engage in learning, learning more-and-more, exercising our minds, therein lies our best future, and not so much in exercising our physical bodies and believing this is the way for staying healthy and alive for a few more days. But if we exercise the muscle of our intellect, then our dreams for the best and their realization are assured. If we are foolish enough to believe we will find health and long life by exercising our muscles, then one day we might be physically strong enough to lift a few hundred pounds over our head, but if we put an equal effort into exercising our intellect, we will be able to lift ourselves and our best dreams up to the stars and beyond. There are no secret kinds of magic hidden within any philosophy, religious or otherwise, which can compete with the magic that changes us, through learning, and with no other magic of any kind, have we even the slightest hope of either surviving as a civilization, a species, or as an individual. Only if we can learn faster than Mother Nature can randomly devise a new test to determine in her way, who shall live, and who shall die-out as either an individual, or as an entire species, then we can survive for another day. Good old Mother Nature loves the diabolical randomness of her own evolutionary crap game, and when she rolls the dice, whatever number comes up, is always the final number for those creatures that haven't yet learned how to survive when their number came up. On more than one of Mother Nature's dice is written our number, the number that points to us as an individual, and the same situation exists for all of Mother Nature's individual creatures. Furthermore, the numbers which represent complete species are all written on her diabolical dice, and Mother Nature's crap game, whose name is evolution, goes on and on, and no individual, or species, ever, under any circumstances, gets excused from playing the game, and in our world of today the only way to quit playing the game, is to die. To continue to survive an individual or a species must win every round of the game, without exception, and if you should loose even one round of the game, then you are dead forever. For our kind to continue to survive we must discover and learn every possible means of forcing the odds for our winning in our favor, instead of in Mother Nature's favor.

It has always been true that living substance is continually evolving, driven by random forces, like a kind of blind unconscious hope which is fueled by nature's fundamental but hidden laws embedded within even the simplest elements of life. Evolution is a force, which pushes and pulls all life forms towards becoming potentially more able to meet the challenges of an unknown future, where unexpected threats or rewards wait hidden behind the future's every corner. It's a future where always some part or parts of the environment are forcibly wrenched into some new reality, and it is all driven by the random interactions of Mother Nature's powerful natural universal forces.

Already existing genetic diversity within a living population has always been for every species, the best insurance for survival against creeping or sudden changes within the natural environment. But by far a more powerful mechanism for our kind's survival, is not nature's slowly evolving genetic diversity, instead for us, it is the diversity of the ideas, which we allow to exist within our sacred information mediums and within our living populations.

What is the substance the essence of this animal that we are? We are not able to find here any immaterial part of us, which is our soul, our eternal spirit, or any part that can now survive beyond the disintegration of our body. But already we, this creature that we are, this animal who is one of the new children of evolution, is asking questions and dreaming dreams, purely spiritual stuff, dreams made of no physical substance, dreams that go beyond the very bounds of time, space, and immortality. Our immortal spirit might now, at last, be in the making.

Where is the one whose walk is like an earthquake upon the landscape? Where is the one who stirs the emotions of the people like some great wind rustling through autumn's leaves? Where is the one whose words fill the air like thunder? Where is this one, who cares and whose loving touch can pluck the strings of harmony to the very depth of human feeling? Where is the one who will make my darkness bright? Where is the one who gives me hope against despair? Where is the one to carry me safely through hard and troubled times to some better and more meaningful future? That one—in every case—is you.

SWINDLE ME LORD, I AM YOUR WILLING SACRIFICE

When con men swindle naive older retired persons out of their money, the money that oftentimes represents their only savings from a lifetime of labors, most everyone who hears about these stories becomes very upset, and they cry out for justice to be done against the thieving con men, but when charlatans, bamboozlers, and clever con men disguise themselves as the prophets, priests, ministers, or evangelists of a religious crusade, and then, when these scheming religious ministers commit the same immoral crimes against the uneducated, the naive, the aged, or poor persons within the general population, the swindlers, those prophets, priests, evangelists, or ministers, are left free to prosper from their relative kind of thievery, and the general population accepts this kind of religious immoral deception without giving a second thought to what has actually transpired. You can find these swindling masquerading prophets, priests, ministers, and evangelists, who are more numerous than grapes in a cluster, crying out their swindling messages from every modern medium of communication. Their messages, mixed with readings from books they personally claim contain god's words, are primarily a plea to send them money, money they desperately require as a means to continue to do the lord's good work, but their messages, which both night and day beg for money, are coupled with near promises, which are partly hidden within contrived and camouflaged wordings, wordings designed to lead the uninitiated in their scheming ways, into believing that they shall receive great rewards for their sacrificial contributions of money. The religious minister's carefully selected words are meant to seem as an almost certain promise that great rewards will soon be coming from their ever thankful god. And the poor, most times those who can least afford to spare even a single coin, are persuaded by words disguised to insinuate a promise of disproportionate returns of both money and/or blessings from the lord, are conned into sending and giving what little money they can spare to these scheming prophets, priest, ministers, and evangelists who sit on golden chairs, and who razzle-dazzle their audience with songs of righteousness, stories of redemption, salvation, forgiveness, and miraculous healings, all designed to beg away the last coin from their mesmerized patrons. It is not beyond these false prophets and proclaimed ministers of the lord, to use false miraculous healings, demonstrated by persons who are willing to exhibit themselves as being physically or mentally stricken, and then to be the object, before a large audience, of the lord's divine personal attention and the supposed total instantaneous miraculous healing of their dubious ills. Supposed miracles abound in these staged dramas, which by means of their emotional play, are designed to convince an audience whose minds are desperate to believe in any promise of salvation, salvation from pain, salvation from crippling, salvation from fears, salvation from unbearable debts, salvation from previous sins, and salvation from eternal death and its grave in the unknown, to convince them that the lord is truly beholden to their disguised unholy cause. Success is the primary word that describes the results from these faked religious drama plays, and success is measured only in terms of the vast amounts of monies that flow into the temple coffers, where behind the temple's curtains the charlatan prophets, priests, evangelists, and ministers wring their hands in excitement and delight over the great treasures they have accumulated, and where on the other side of the temple's curtain of deception, those poor souls who were the original owners of part of that treasure are left poorer in every way than before, because without the slightest mercy for their situation, they were coaxed, by the fakers, into sacrificing what very little they had. But there are also those, whose financial status is not that of desperation, and they are also swindled into contributing to the temple coffers, and after contributing they are not noticeably financially different from what they were before, but they feel they have possibly bought some edge against the unknown elements that are preached to exist and might be threatening to them if they did not contribute to the temple's stock.

The God of Creation does not want those ignorant and disordered creatures, whose minds have been poisoned with false ideas, the very ones that evangelist, ministers, preachers, and false prophets call forth in god's name, only the religious extremists want them for the one or two coins of money they might donate to support their extreme views, and out of the world's most poor, and mentally crippled creatures, the religious extremists suck up their follower's last blood and their last coin, and deftly con them into giving blind political support to candidates who have little intellectual substance to offer the political system and then they lead these weak souls on like blind creatures, and promise them paradise after their death, and promise a sure forgiveness of their sins. Not only do the religious false prophets use their follower's few monies to build a religious system whose fundamental base is financial power, but they also use their follower's blind and ignorant obedience, and the power base represented by their shear numbers to wield evermore power and to use that power as a means of infringing on the basic nature of the political system, and therefore ultimately to the detriment of any ideas that are different from their own primitive closed minded views of the world.

There are those religious fanatics, the faithful believers in the literal interpretation of the unholy holy books, who are actively involved in censoring the public's freedom of access to information that within their confused and narrow minds they see as forbidden knowledge. Religious fanatics hide their sick and monstrous intent while they seep onto board's of educations, library committees, and local governments as a means of infiltrating their fundamentalist religiously biased ideas to control the decisions of these institutions. Some individual religious fanatics practice their own form of terrorism upon unsuspecting public libraries by checking out or sometimes directly stealing books and other materials that they consider should be forbidden, and they either simply never return the books to the library, or they destroy them.

THE UNHOLY HOLY BOOKS

Religious differences are as powerful of barriers
between peoples and the free exchange of ideas, as
mountains, deserts, and rivers are powerful barriers
between nations

The various different religious holy books are with out doubt; the best
selling and least voluntarily read best-selling books in the world. They
are the books that contain the world's largest collection of near-truths,
half-truths, and outright lies. These so called holy writings are all relics
from a distant time, a time, not unlike our present time, when the most
unbelievable dramatic and theatrical exaggerations were the chosen
methods for falsely tying their god or gods into a direct interaction with
their own mortal heroes, or their village, tribe, or nation's historical
struggles. In all of these writings we find, what to any educated and
rational mind, are the most illogical and patently ridiculous claims of a
god's interactions with their chosen people's long past supposed historical events. These miraculous interventions of their god are of course

told in what was, at the time of the story's telling and its much later written record, believable terms. Terms, which clearly reveal how little the storytellers knew of the real world and the rest of the universe that surrounded it. The stories are told in terms, which would surly cause any knowing god to buckle over with laughter, but they were terms acceptable to a people, who were willing in their ignorance to believe in every fictional tale of ghosts, angels, devils, black magic, sorcerer's healings, and any and every kind of invisible mystic contrivance, which the storytellers purported to in fact be true, and the story's supposed truths were validated by the testimonies of one ignorant and willing testifier after another.

Some of these stories are of what at a first cursory reading describe powerful acts by the people's god, such as in one instance, the parting of the waters of a sea, so that "Their God's chosen and righteous people" could escape, through a sea's opened passage, from a powerful phantom army that was purported to be in their pursuit. A far more dangerous obstacle to "God's chosen and righteous people," and an element that is far more difficult to traverse than any of the sea's waters is the more than eight feet of sedimentary mud which covers the sea's bottom. Of course the storytellers of the time didn't know of the mud's existence, nor apparently did their god, for this most important mud, their god failed to clear from the passage across the bottom of the sea, and the story's writers fail to mention any words about any miraculous clearing of mud. Today's religious manipulators of holy book histories work diligently at attempting to find plausible explanations of how their particular god used some force of nature, the force of the wind to separate the waters of the sea, whose bottom was falsely proclaimed as dry, but none of them have yet proposed any divine bulldozers to clear away that damn mud.

Realize that the storyteller's ever guiding desire was to establish their people's, their tribe's, and their nation's place in history as being the most notable and special above all other peoples. It is the flamboyantly exaggerated stories of those storytellers, which were later compiled and written as a true history into the unholy holy books. There we can see the storytellers technique for establishing the greatness of their nation's history, history as the storytellers claimed it to be, and whose stories directly linked the people and their history with the power of some great and protecting god, a god who had personally guided them through difficult times and delivered them as survivors that had escaped from one unbelievable and seemingly inescapable crises after another. The very bread, oils, meat, and cheese, which was needed to feed the storyteller and his family, was derived solely from the audiences that were willing to listen to the storyteller's stories and to pay him for their being entertained. The storytellers of the time had the strongest of incentives to contrive their stories to be the most amazing in everyway and with a little or a complete disregard for the truth, and in those days, as well as now, stories of some god's miraculous interactions with mere humans, or unusual sexual intrigues among royalty, were and are always the best selling of stories. And so it has come to pass that the unholy holy books that have survived from ancient times are primarily filled with these storyteller's best original or plagiarized stories of some mortal people's direct relationship with a god. Now days, the best characterization of this kind of writing is not named "Holy," but instead is named "A Fictional Historical Novel."

The unholy holy stories and writings from long past yesterdays, present to us as fact, tales of miraculous healings, whose individual numbers can be nearly counted in a one-to-one correspondence to your own fingers and toes. The unholy holy book's stories contain tales of miraculous healings of what in their time were incurable maladies. Sadly for most persons, these supposed miraculous cures, were not at that time made available to the general population. The miraculous cures were in fact supposed to be the unholy holy book's window display of what was, or might be available, if a person was a devout believer in the unholy holy book's hocus-pocus, and if they were an unwavering follower of the unholy holy book's institutionalized interpreters, care-takers, and priests.

Base on the various unholy holy books' few advertised miraculous cures of incurable maladies, many people of today's world profess to be astounded at these purported religious medical miracles, and in response they give their solemn obedience to those religions, whose miracle workers are purported to have worked the magic of the cures. This seems to be the most monumental case of making a mountain out of a mini-molehill that any ridiculously imaginative mind could possibly conjure up. Every single day, without exception, day-in and day-out, those persons of the modern medical profession perform a thousand times more medical miracles than the sum total of all the miracles performed by all of religion's prophets, healers, and supposed miracle workers throughout all of recorded religious history. But you don't see the religious leaders directing their followers to offer up their praise, prayers, and blessings at the doorways of modern medicine, even though, it is there were thousands upon thousands of healing miracles are each day to be found, real miracles, proven miracles, even the raising of the dead. But then, the "true" religious believer has never been able to be persuaded by facts, even when millions upon millions of facts are staring them directly in the face. The true believer is more likely, in their near blind obedience to their religious faith, always to see their tiny molehills as the giant mountains, even when real mountains of verifiable truths are piled around them to heights of tens of thousands of feet in altitude, and such is a part of the basic blind nature of those with contagious poisoned minds.

In the distant past there were those certain persons who very much liked to wander off into the wilderness and while there, they would fast and nearly starve themselves to death. Then while they were in this exhausted and isolated state of mind, they would come to believe that they were having a religious experience where devils, angels, or their god would appear to them in reality or in a vision. Sometimes while in these lack of nourishment induced states of mind, they would believe they had received divine directives and commandments. You can be assured that if you go out into the wilderness and sufficiently starve yourself, you can also have your own hallucinatory religious experiences. Here we note, their will probably be a difference about your hallucinatory experience, and that is, you will understand the cause, but ancient peoples did not understand the cause of their wonderful euphoric hallucinations, and they sincerely did believe that the personages of their dreams and hallucinations were true and real. And so today we name those ancient people who voluntarily sugar starved their brains "Prophets."

The true believer's most revered prophets, as described within the different unholy holy books, each have stories of their lives, wherein at their earthly life's ending, the prophet does not ever just simply die, as all other persons who have ever lived on Earth, just simply die. Instead the so-called prophets are, at the final ending of their lives, lifted up in one way or another, by accompanying angles or maybe on a magical flying horse, or sometimes with their own sprouted angel's wings, and they supposedly ascend to an open gated heaven, where they are purported to have been received among a heavenly assembly presided over by the one-and-only great god. In the real world we have not been so fortunate as to have caught even one falling feather from those supposed lifting angelic wings, nor has anyone at the time of any profit's great escape from Earth been lucky enough to have been hit on the head with any other free falling sacred substances, although throughout the tales within the unholy holy books there is plenty of that scattered about to at least make that part of the stories believable.

For some of the peoples who faithfully and blindly believe in the substance of their unholy holy books, one belief of a primary consequence, is the belief that their particular god smiles on, and rewards those peoples and those nations, who know the secret ways of their god, and know exactly how their god demands to be worshiped. They know

exactly when and what prayers and sacrifices are required, what fasting
and rituals will please their god, when and what treks to various religious shines are required by their god. The people believe that by their
doing of these prescribed things, their god will be pleased and will smile
down upon them and rain their god's bounteous blessings upon the
peoples and the nations that rigorously honor god's need to be worship
in exact accordance with the specific requirements written in their holy
books. And when no great blessings are forthcoming from their god,
many of the faithful followers of the written holy word, become
absolutely enraged. And when they see that peoples other than those of
their beliefs are continually reaping bountiful rewards of every imaginable variety and kind, and that the highly desirable commodities of
milk and honey are so abundantly plentiful to others who have different
beliefs, they become confused and outraged, when they see that these
commodities are literally overflowing from those other nation's boarders. And when in their rage, they see, that others than they are reaping
all of the benefits, which they believed should be coming to them as a
result of the faithful obedience to the words of their god. And to their
great dismay they see that amongst their true believers, their lives are
mostly dominated, instead of by the bounties of nature, with illiteracy,
poverty, sickness, ignorance, early death, and a long list of immedicable
sufferings. And some of the people begin to meditate, and to solemnly
ponder as to what their peoples might have done wrong to displease
their god that their god would forsake them by not rewarding them in
equal or better measure than those who believed differently from them,
and who follow a different guidance. And from the smoke of their pon-
derings and sincere meditations they arrive at the conclusion that they
must not be following their holy book's words to its most exact meaning. So to improve their situation, many of their peoples become fanat-
ical about interpreting, in the most exacting terms, their holy book's
words. And these fanatics will not allow for any deviation, even ever so
slightly, from what is interpreted as the literal meaning of the holy

book's doctrine. When any people takes up any such a rigid religious doctrinal philosophy, they become absolute religious fundamentalists, and the historical evidence clearly shows this religious fundamentalism eventually and inevitably leads to a disaster in the social structure that drives the society and every part of the culture in an ever downward spiral, whose only end is desperate despair. Then the other peoples of the world become both witness and targets of a hateful revenge as the final frustrated fundamental madness flings its uncontrollable rage, at seeing its own ultimate disastrous failures, at those who are of any different belief. And behold you have our world of today.

Religions have proven over-and-over again that they can take a most promising and hopeful time, and miraculously change it into a time where the people suffer from every misery of the mind and body that can ever be imagined.

WAR

Without exception there are no other human endeavors that can compare in their gross ignorance and shear stupidity to the human endeavor named "War." To finally rid ourselves from this most unreasonable of human behaviors, we must replace the "bloodletting" kind of war, with wars that are to our common advantage, wars that are beneficial to all, except for those few who now greatly prosper by supplying the means to conduct wars of destruction, bloodletting, maiming, and death. The time has arrived when the only wars we should conduct are a sustained war against our common real enemies, intolerance, disease, ignorance, bigotry, and unnatural synthetic bonds upon our free creative spirit.

It is at least minimally stupid to even consider making war against any and every perceived threat from a foreign power, when we, all of us, have more sinister and deadly threats to every aspect of our persons and to our society than is any foreign power. We have enemies right among us that every day, every month, and every year, cripple our bodies, rack us with intolerable pain, stalk us mercilessly and force us into an unwelcome grave. These enemies that thrive among us, slaughter us, and we die in their demon hands, tens of thousands is the number of our fallen friends and family members who perish each and every year, year-in and year-out. Yet we idiotically look at foreign threats as our worst enemy, foreign enemies are in every aspect miniscule when compared to those invisible enemies every day thriving within our midst. These domestic enemies break our bones, immobilize our body's joints, crumble our teeth, rob us of our precious memories, and break us down bit-by-bit, inch-by-inch, until they, the invisible enemies, are our domineering masters, and pain is the tax we daily pay to them as our sacrificial offering, while they beat us down and rob us of our pride and of our human dignity. We, all of us, are every day paying the tax of fear and pain, and we willingly pay it, because from day-to-day, life at nearly any cost seems pregnant with a hope of surviving for another day, and almost any kind of life seems better than the hells that religions have fictitiously conjured up and indoctrinated into believing young minds, and those frightening hallucinations of a conjured up hell stalk our thoughts in the back of our minds and we are fearful of what might await us in the unknown beyond. And so we are willing to be tortured by life's most outrageously cruel invisible villains in hopes of living for one more day, one more hour, or one more minute because of our never ending hope that just around the next corner of time lies our salvation.

We are willing to sacrifice vast fortunes of time and money on warring against foreign countries whose threats are generally feeble things, when they are honestly compared to those terrible threats that daily thrive among us. It must become our fervent first choice to direct our time and fortunes into an all-out war effort against the enemies among us, which by the vast number of their victims and the savageness of their crimes should clearly designates them as our enemies of first priority.

We need to make a concerted effort, a kind of war, against the villainous hidden monsters that are burrowed into the laws that govern our economic rules and the lack of morals of some uncaring persons who hide beneath the fallen leaf clutter of a thousand petty economic laws, where is hidden economic advantages not meant to be seen by moral eyes. We need to closely examine how extreme opulence, opulence beyond anyone's wildest dreamt of needs, is seen as a moral and a natural and desirable consequence of the economic system, while the desperate needs of hundreds of thousands of persons are left wanting of any remedy. We need to make a serious war to understand the machinery of our economic system and once the detailed reality of the system is known, we then must modify those parts of the mechanism that allow it to drift so far from what is clearly both right, just, and moral. So many privileged individuals now are feeding at this trough of economic immorality, that the effort to make the changes necessary to repair the economic system must not be left in their power corrupted hands, but should first find its means in courts of justice, of common justice, not of privileged justice.

We need to make war against the bandaged and patched together education system of the past, whose body has been dragged into the present day, where it delivers less than our best hopes for our children's understanding and for guiding them towards finding meaning, happiness, and success in life. Scattered through out the world are the individual proven successful and workable ideas, that when brought together can give us a better educational system that fits the needs of both the student and of the society.

We need to make a serious and concerted war against those laws, where the evidence clearly demonstrates, except to those near blind and indoctrinated politicians who were the law's instigators, that some laws are more of a detriment to our people and our society than they are of any imaginable possible benefit.

We need in some instances to logically rethink the morality of "The end cannot justify the means" and come to realize that in many situations it is a moral fact that the "End can many times be a justification of the means taken to achieve that end." We during a time of war are often faced with making the decision of whether or not to send our beloved young Marines into a battle where it is certain that most of them will surely loose their lives, but the cry from those who stand safely on the sidelines, is always "Send in the Marines" and the justification is that the Marines, by sacrificing their lives are protecting our nation and its ways of life. And so here we can see that there are times where by means of sacrificing some lives in battle; we consider it to be morally right, if the sacrifice protects the nation from further threats. So now I ask you to consider the condition that is becoming prevalent throughout the world and each day is a growing threat to everyone's society and to civilization itself, and that condition is the growing threat to everyone from those, who for one reason or another choose to unleash terrible violence upon innocent unsuspecting, unprotected citizens. It is of an immediate concern that acts of terrorism initialed by individuals or by organizations be stopped. And if we sincerely want to put a final end to terrorism, then we must abandon our childish approach at solving this lingering and dangerous problem where hidden phantoms can lurk within any dark shadow from where they can spring at any time to reck havoc and death upon innocent people who are going about their civilized life. We must be deadly realistic at designing our solution to ending these problems perpetrated by mad people with sick poisoned minds. We must instigate a powerful philosophy, whose root ideas are equivalent to the root ideas of the evil we wish to end, and which might appear at first reckoning, as a seemingly irrational and immoral proposal for stopping terrorism of every form, including religious instigated terrorism, there is one, and only one certain and sure way of doing it. This way may seem to be against the moral fabric of most so-called civilized societies, but the conclusion of this method's application will be the effective defeat of most all terrorist activities—the method is simple—cruel—and most effective. The method is this, for each and every victim of any terrorist's attack, the society that has been attacked is given an international sanction to search out to locate every family member, friend, or associate of the terrorist or terrorists who made the attack, and to kill, their family members, friends, or associates, in a one to one correspondence to the number of victims who died because of the terrorist's attack. It is a kind of harshest application of the ancient unholy holy book's laws of equality of crime and punishment. The order of the killing should be of the terrorist's closest relatives first, father, mother, sisters, brothers, aunts, uncles, nephews, nieces, and so on. If not enough family members can be found to satisfy the needs of a one-on-one retribution, then the terrorist's closest friends should then be killed, and if there are not enough friends to satisfy the numerical needs of equal retribution, then anyone who was an associate of the terrorist should be killed until the total number killed in revenge satisfies the numerical equality of those who died from the original crime. What in the final reality is prescribed by this method, is only what is proposed by a fundamental interpretation of the unholy holy books, and the method is a just and moral means for nipping this plague of terrorism in its bloody bud, and to put a final end to this next greatest of all unholy crimes against civilized peoples.

By examining our past and our recent history, it becomes most obvious that our kind has acted like a ruthless beast, whose emerging consciousness was still a primitive mechanism only slightly better than that of many other creatures. We can see the ruthless animal that were are, by looking at the details of the major wars and other battles we have fought, and by seeing the staggering number of men, women and children that have been minced on those battle fields. It is long past the time where other than claiming our supremacy above and beyond that of every other animal by means of forever pointing to our numerous technological accomplishments, that we look instead to our long history of pain, destruction, and death which we have rained upon our own kind in a continuous manner, since we first became the self named masters of the scene, where we can see we are more of a vicious primitive animal than is any other animal in nature's garden. If we continue to be the primitive animal that we were when we first became conscious thinking creatures, then it is late for our kind. It is time we actually stood fully upright, and begin dealing with our own kind and the other creatures of creation in a manner which the God of Creation has given us the foresight to see is truly good, and will yield up a better world for us all. Now is the time, instead of wallowing in our political and economic miseries and making war on our own kind, now is the time to put an end to all of this costly and illogical nonsense, which we have been engaged in since we were first barely able to think and create our own dreams of what might be better than what we have. Now is the time to take hold of those great new tools of science, the arts, and technology and use them to burst into a future that is better than any of us has ever known, better for all persons and not just the select few and a future where bloody war against our own kind is a thing lost in the past.

THE ARTS

From early times, the mythologies of religious doctrine have been so divorced from verifiable reality, that they existed as mere hallucinations, which hung as ghostly forms within religious minds, minds which were barely able to connect with reality. In such a nebulous state, the mythologies could not alone on their substance of nothingness, survive. They needed some blood of reality, or near reality, to give them some strength of belief. Their only hope for sustained survival was that they be given some physical substance, which could be presented as real truth; so that the eyes, ears, and touch could believe it all was real. And it came to pass that the Arts were commanded to give these ghosts of the mind, some embellishments, glorious bodies, clothes, and all of those things that are recognizable as substances of the real would. The mythologies were embellished with fascinating, powerful, and cleverly devised stories, with statues representing their supposed form, and paintings to confirm their mythical exploits. The wonderful ever growing world of embellishments, which falsely testifies to the truth of religion's all, is to this very day, so vastly grown, and are so enormous, and are of such a beautiful and spectacular display, that they perfectly hide beneath the tonnage of their, constructed, sculpted, painted, and storied weight, the lies at the center of all the fuss.

Near to the heart of human kind sits, like some ragged unwanted Cinderella stepchild, the Arts and Artist of our kind. The Arts whose true awesome power is second not even to science. The Arts whose very soul is the unheralded other voice of our kind. The Arts that vibrate meaning from any and every medium. The Arts whose mighty power has for all of time been bound and hidden, an invisible Prometheus from whose captured body, the mystic philosophies have carefully squeezed like tooth paste, "The Cream of Created Reality," to make fantasy fact, and falsehoods believable, and to rebottle the lie and to present it as historical truth. The Arts whose immobilized body has with economic torture yielded to paint history as it never was. The Arts whose awesome power has with shameful humility bowed to weaker philosophies. The Arts whose gentle hands have led us with some dignity through blind and troubled times. The Arts whose hands can pluck in everyway the hidden strings of our deepest emotions. The Arts whose every action is freedom's flesh in motion. The Arts whose shrine-doors swing open only be the levers of the currency of the time and thereby allow us a brief moment of worship, and we pay our tribute with an individual's coin of true value, smiles, laughter, frowns, and tears of sadness or joy, and new understandings, which too, too seldom, are coaxed from the purse of the most inner being. For the peoples that really love this giant, unties its bonds, heals its wounds, succors it to full life, and wins its love, they shall not win just the laurels of the day, the triumphs through time shall be theirs

The arts because of their unique and most powerful magic of gentle persuasion, owe to us, to society, as a kind of near holy sacrifice of their creative talents, a sacrifice to help us discover believable paths leading from where we find ourselves in the present to some better future. The Arts must help us to visualize by the means of the art's various mediums, a world of tomorrow which is clearly better than today's world. They owe such an effort to those many of us who willingly cast some of our treasure to their shrines. We their followers, their hopeful patrons, deserve some good, their best, in return for our worship of their works. There was a time, in the not so distant past, when motion pictures often showed to us images of some lifestyle that was believable, but just beyond those things and comforts of our common simple lives. They showed us lifestyles that we did not know from our own experiences. They showed us magnificent movie sets, beautiful clothes, life styles in a world of plenty, happy times, new music and dancing, they showed us a world that was not impossible for us to obtain if we discovered that we liked and desired it. They showed us a world we could believe might become real, because we had seen it with our own eyes on the theater's screen. And that world, which at that time was only a dream on film, we obtained for ourselves, and continued, by means of the Art's ignited hope within us, to attain the comforts of today's world, which for many persons living within a prosperous nation far exceeds the comforts, and well being of any and all past kings of the Earth. It is the Arts, more than any other institution, which can ignite our imagination and stimulate us to dream the best we can dream. No one should ever even suggest that the direction any of the Arts choose as their path, should be dictated by any person or group, or censored in anyway. But the Artists should be reminded that they have a responsibility, because of their unique position of power, to sometimes use that power to explore and help us to see whatever might be to our advantage, to know, and to understand.

THE EVIDENCE OF
RELIGION'S DECLINE

Here is told a synoptic story that is detailed enough to reveal the past and the awesome power of some of its dominant religions. Hopefully it will become evident by examining the structures and the mechanisms for maintaining religious power, that from the most ancient of times until today, religion's absolute dominance over the lives of the people has grown weaker-and-weaker as the people gained more-and-more knowledge, which directly contradicted the teachings of their religion. With the gaining of knowledge, the people also gained the will to stand up against the religious leaders and their prescribed unholy holy doctrines. By the power of growth in the number of enlightened people and their evolving newly found knowledge, the people have become more-and-more strongly resolved not to allow the priest of any religion to offer human victims as a sacrifice to any god.

We here pause and look back in time, to glimpse for a few moments religion's darkest most powerful past. There we shall see the historical fragments, here ordered from their most powerful of times to the most recent evidence of their declining power. First, we can see and understand just how powerful were some of the past's religions as exemplified by three primary aspects of their power, which are able to speak to us from across time's barrier of long past centuries, and to speak directly to our reason and our logic. These three, the holy trinity of facts, bear their evidence, first through the surviving remains of enormous constructions, which the religions of the time commanded to be built, secondly by the vast number of followers, which they could command to do their bidding, and thirdly, and a more important direct indicator, in some cases, of their awesome power, is revealed by the unrestrained savagery they could wield against anyone they chose to sacrifice, and by the extraordinary and inhumane nature of their different sacrifices. We will see what religions were once like, and if unrestrained, just how powerful they could again become.

Clearly understand that when the people were called by the ancient priests to witness the ceremonies or sacrifices to some god, the people, driven by fear, obediently came as they were commanded, and they obediently witnessed all that was performed, but during these times the people were assembled as witnesses, they had a powerful fear within their hearts, it was a monumental fear, which had been implanted within their minds during a lifetime of bearing witness to the savage and brutal ritual sacrifices to their religion's gods. The common people held fear of both the god's priests, and of the gods themselves, for the gods of those times were ever more real, and ever more believable to the people of their time, than the gods of today's religions are believable to the peoples of today.

All religions have steadily been loosing their power for controlling the common people's lives, even thought the number of their members might be increasing, and so now, one of religion's primary strategies is to gain power by financial means. Ever since the dawn of intellect and the dawn of science, the power of the world's religions has been on a steady decline. In the beginning, when religions were at the peak of their power, they controlled every aspect of society and of the lives of all of the individual's within that society. When ancient religions were at the height of their power, their call would bring into an assembly a hundred thousand or more eager god-fearing persons to meet whatever demands were laid upon them. This is evidenced by the size of the great ancient ceremonial and sacrificial sites dotted here and there upon the world's continents. Some of these ceremonial sites could only be constructed, in ancient times, by means of using vast numbers of human laborers to cleave from the Earth and move enormous pieces of stone to the religious ceremonial site's location. Even without written evidence, these most ancient religious sites, which have been constructed by assembling giant sized stones, makes is clear that the power of the religions, which ordered these constructions, was ominous.

When we look to Egypt, we see religious monuments of such extraordinary size and beauty that they speak clearly and directly as a voice from the past, of the power of those who commanded their construction. The vast religious monuments of ancient Egypt reveals to us a most unusual story as compared to most other societies of the past, which also were dominated by religion. But ancient Egypt was an unusual land, which contained what was during ancient times, the most valuable of all resources, fertile soil, an unending source for fresh water, and a powerful natural protection, provided by the extensive and nearly unbreachable desert barriers on both sides of the Nile River. This desert barrier protected Egypt's resources and the ancient culture that grew up and flourished along the length of the great river. It is the productivity of agriculture, which is the basic foundation of power within any and every ancient and most modern societies. In ancient Egypt, the overwhelming success of agricultural productivity is directly reflected in the number of religious monuments, their sometimes-gigantic size, and their extraordinary simple beauty, all of which testify to the enormous influence religion had upon the lives of Egypt's peoples. What is, in general, quite different from most other religious controlled ancient societies is that the sacrifices offered to Egypt's many gods and to the people's loved ones who had died, were not sacrifices of humans, or of human blood, which are the kinds of typical sacrifices demanded by most all of the powerful ancient religions, whose ultimate purpose was to command obedience by means of striking fear into the hearts of the people, fear of their gods and fear of those priests who were self declared representatives for the gods. But the sacrificial offerings to the dead and the gods of ancient Egypt were the simple commodities needed to sustain the people's own lives. The Egyptians offered as their sacrifice food and drink and useful utility tools common to the people's own daily needs in life. It seems that within an ancient society where the needs of life are in an over abundant supply and the population feels safe from the threats, which normally come from coveting neighboring societies, then there is no need for human sacrifices as a means of establishing a great controlling fear in the people. The religions of ancient Egypt, which were directly married to the government, had control over the people, not by fear of torture or human sacrifice, but by the means of a total control over the entire surplus of food. Ancient Egyptians were not driven or forced by fear of religious retribution into building their vast monuments, but they voluntarily built them, because in the simplicity of their understanding of life, they believed in the reality of their gods and of their god kings. It was, as their monumental structures bear silent witness, the people's belief that what they constructed was a means of obtaining immortality, eternal life, this they most sincerely believed. When the ancient Egyptians were called by their religious authorities to build their monumental structures, they came by the tens of thousands to do this work, and they willingly labored at these constructions for thirty or forty years or until the structure was completed and such were the people's religious tasks for more than three thousand years. Here in the surviving monuments of ancient Egypt is the clear evidence of a religious power of such a devout enormity, yet such a great and somewhat benevolent religious power has never since been seen.

From the earliest of times the most dominant of reoccurring visual mysteries, where those that demanded some explanation of the nature of the sun, moon, rain, wind, or fire. As concerns the nature of the sun and of the moon one of the most puzzling and frightening questions, which demanded immediate explanation, was where do these powerful presences of nature disappear to during nighttime for the sun, and daytime for the moon, although sometimes a ghost of the moon can be seen creeping across the day's blue sky. These natural object mysteries became the incorporated spirits and gods of our kind's first religions, gods whose power over the people was absolute, unquestionable, and ever-demanding of obedience and of sacrifices to placate any and every of these god's whimsical desires. These gods embodied in natural phenomenon were so powerful in the eyes of the common people that they dominated as the primary gods of all religions throughout the world for thousands of years.

We see from the physical evidence, located at Teotihuacan in Mexico, the unbelievably huge ceremonial site, whose area for religious assemblage is beyond that of most other religious ceremonial sites of the ancient or modern world. We see here, the great temple of the Sun God and the temple of the Moon God, which are positioned along the site's grand plaza. We see at this vast site, which covers more than twelve square miles, more than two thousand dwellings, and along the length of its infamous "Avenue of the Dead," there were more than a hundred individual religious shrines each dedicated to one of the numerous gods. Almost nothing is, with certainty, known about the peoples who constructed this single enormous religious ceremonial site, but there should be little doubt that the religious leaders, who called for its construction, wielded a power over their people that was surely as great for its place and time as any that has ever been demonstrated. For reasons unknown, Teotihuacan became suddenly abandoned and the archeological evidence reveals, all of its religious shrines had been put to the torch.

The other evidence which we need to consider, other that the huge physical religious ceremonial constructions, which by their presence indicates the power held by the religious leaders who commanded their construction, is the awesome power over the people, which can be understood by investigating the nature of the sacrifices, which the religion's leaders were able to successfully demand from their followers. We can also gain an insight into the might of religious power by looking at the masses of people who obediently assemble when they were called to worship and to see the sacrifices offered up to their gods.

From the ancient temples of what was then the island city of Tenochtitlan in Mexico, we have in some instances direct eye witness knowledge of the nearly unbelievable power of a religion and its priest's domination of their people's lives by means of inspiring religious doctrinal fear into the people's hearts, literally into their hearts. But outside of their society's religious beliefs, the Aztecs during the fourteenth and fifteenth centuries ruled their empire in a logical, well regulated, and otherwise seemingly civilized manner. The Aztec's center of both civil and religious power was at Tenochtitlan, present day Mexico City. The governing officials who controlled the daily activities within the empire were efficient and effective at running a well-organized and stable society. But there was a strong absolutely inseparable inner-tie at every level of the Mexican, Aztec, government's functioning and their religion, which yielded up a monstrously powerful controlling fear that dominated the Mexican people's lives, the Aztec people's lives. Here within a otherwise seemingly civilized city, and throughout the Aztec empire, existed a religion, whose primary power over the people was derived from monstrous fear and inhuman human sacrifices, coupled with never ending demands for self-torture by the means of personal ritualized blood letting. The religion had many proscribed methods for sacrificing to their various gods including: The cutting out of the heart from a live human sacrificial victim, or throwing a live human sacrificial victim onto a flaming brazier, or the beheading of women while they were performing a religious ritual dance, or the slitting of a human sacrificial victim's throat, or by ritual drowning, or strangulation, or ritually beating the victim to death, or crushing the human sacrificial victim with rocks and then locking him up to suffer until death came, these are but a few of the hideous methods employed in making ritual human sacrifices to various Aztec gods and as the religion's means of striking obedient fear into the minds of the population.

But to give some minimal relief to the Aztec people's fears, most of sacrificial victims where chosen from the vast numbers of health young enemy warriors, who had been captured during battles and were temporarily held in captivity. War was frequently made, and one of its primary purposes was to capture young healthy enemy male combatants, as a means of providing a never-ending supply of humans who would later become sacrificial offerings to the Aztec's gods.

The Aztecs had many gods; two of their most powerful gods were Huitzilopotchtli the god of the sun and war, and another god Tlaloc, the god of rain and all watery things and also of fertility. The Aztecs built a pyramid temple, for their gods Huitzilopotchtli and Tlaloc, in their capital city Tenochtitlan. At first the temple was a humble edifice made of sticks and reeds, but as the power of the religion grew, so did the size and splendor of the temple grow. Over the two hundred years of the Aztec empire's existence, the temple was enlarged many times, and at the completion of each remodeling, mass sacrifices of human hearts and blood were offered up to the gods, in a brutal ceremony that went on for days-upon-days. The final from of the great pyramid temple was meant to represent the holy mountain on which their god Huitzilopotchtli was supposedly born, and the height of the temple was meant to touch the clouds, which were one part of the domain of their rain god Tlaloc. Unlike the religions of today, who secretly dream of dominating the world by means of fear and force, it was said the god Huitzilopotchtli, openly and boldly boasted to his priests and people, "We shall conquer all of the universe." and he also boasted, "I will make my priests, lords and kings of every place in the world," which is also a common behind the scenes hope of religious leaders today. The great temple in its final glory, before the Spaniards conquered the Aztec's Empire, had at its apex a separate shrine for each of the two prime gods. On the West side of the temple pyramid, more than a hundred stone steps formed an ascending steep stairway, which led upward from site's ground-level ceremonial plaza, to the top of the pyramid, where sacrificial alters stood in front of the god's sanctuaries. The rock base of the pyramid temple was carved all around with the images of giant fear inspiring snakes. At appointed times, on a regular schedule, which were set out in the religious doctrine, or at special times designated by the priests, the priests made sacrifices to the gods by cutting and tearing out the beating hearts from living male sacrificial victims. At the top of the temple, in plain view of the people assembled below in the plaza, were the god's sacrificial alters, each a large arched stone designed to present the victim in a posture which made their living body most easily accessible to the tools of ritual sacrifice. The victim was laid with his back arched across the alter and with his abdomen and ribs arch up, four priests held and spread out each of the victims arms and legs. Then while the human sacrifice struggled and squirmed to get free, the high priest with the ritual sacrificial obsidian knife in his hand, cut and sawed through the victim's lower chest's muscular diaphragm, then the priest forcibly reached up inside the struggling victim's hot and bleeding chest cavity, and with one hand and arm inside the hot living sacrifice, the priest grabbed and clutched the victim's living heart, and with the sharp and jagged obsidian knife in his other hand, he forcibly plunged again into the victim's chest cavity and sawed, cut, and hacked the living heart away from its convulsing arteries and veins which had connected it to the sacrificial victim's living body. The priest pulled the still beating heart from the body, and held it up for the statue of the god to behold the still throbbing human heart, which was offered in holy sacrifice. The dead body of the sacrificial victim was carried to the edge of the steep stone stairway that looked down to the plaza below, and without sympathy the body was thrown down the temple's steps, where it oozed out its last bit of sacred blood to add to the slow flowing streams of blood, which mingled with the blood from previous human sacrifices of the day's offerings to the all powerful gods, their priests, and to satisfy the doctrine of their religion.

Young children were sometimes sacrificed, by the priests to the god Tlaloc, in the belief that their flowing tears would bribe the god into delivering rain.

Some kind of blood sacrifice was required daily as the only means of giving the sun god the energy to make its daily journey across the sky.

For the common people, both the truth and the power of their religion was an undeniable fact as seen before their very eyes, each and every day some blood sacrifice was made to the sun god, and each and every day the people were witnesses to the success of these offerings, as the sun did each and every day make its journey safely across the sky. And the people were also witnesses to the absolute success of the sacrificial offerings to the rain god Tlaloc, for when the offerings to the god did not immediately bring rain, then the priests continued to make evermore-significant sacrificial offerings to the god, and of course rain always finally came. So the people had powerful, believable, real world evidence in the power of their gods, which they so much reverenced and feared. "Fear your lord god" and they did.

Cruel, devilish, and frightful human sacrifice was the bribe the gods required in return for their granting to their people, good health, rain, good harvests, and military success.

Here is one last look, so that you might more completely understand the nearly unbelievable and horrible scope of this most powerful unholy holy religion. When the last enlargement of the Tenochtitlan temple, at Mexico City, was completed, on the next day, and before the morning's sunrise, four lines of men, victims, waiting to become sacrificial offerings, stood one after another and each one of the four lines stretched, from the temple's steps in the plaza, for more than two and one half miles along the four causeways which connected the island city of Tenochtitlan to its lake's shores. It took the priests four days to sacrifice all of the victims, multitudes of priests worked in shifts at the hard labor of cutting out the living hearts from the god's sacrificial offerings. More than ten thousand human sacrifices were made, every minute two beating hearts were hacked from the living victim's bodies. Blood literally ran in rivers down the temple's steps and pooled in a huge lake of human blood in the plaza at the temple's base. You might here believe that we have told a tale that has conveyed the worst of the story of this most powerful religion, but history knows we have only revealed the smallest part of this whole unbelievable two hundred year story of savageness, a story almost beyond belief.

The Aztec's world in many ways was not unlike today's world, where the most startling contradictions between daily life and religious beliefs exist in the mind side-by-side as the strangest kind of a mutually embarrassed insanity. It is the natural heart of insanity that the insane are not able to separate those things whose real existence is detectable by the body's senses from those things that are solely conjured up by the imagination, and where the ghosts born solely from imagination dominate every day. People who are religious are not mentally well connected with reality—and the more religious they are—then the less well are they connected to reality. And if they are overly religious, then they are so detached from reality that society declares they are insane and locks them away, in a place where they can receive psychiatric treatment in an attempt to relieve their mad delusions. Sometimes when persons are religious enough to be declared delusional, but they somehow escape from being diagnosed, and are left to run freely in society, we soon see some of those persons demonstrating in the most extreme ways the absurdity of their beliefs, such as throwing their family off from some great height from which they fall to their deaths, infants first, then the older children, then in culmination to this insane act, the parent jumps to their own death. All of this, in the foolish belief that they would immediately find themselves happily together in their god's heaven, when instead they are all there together, smashed, broken, and dead, all over the concrete of a public sidewalk.

A belief of many of the today's religions, and a similar kind of belief, that was commonly accepted by the Aztecs, was that the spirits, of those Aztec warriors who died in battle, traveled straight away to an Eastern Paradise to become attendants to the sun god, a place from where the deceased warrior's spirits accompanied and protected the sun god during the time of the god's, the sun's, first morning rising until the god had traveled to the middle of the day's sky, then from there other escorts accompanied the sun god on his journey to his evening's setting. After four years of daily traveling with and protecting the sun god, the warrior's spirits were allowed to return to Earth as humming birds, or as other birds, or butterflies, who were allowed to pluck honey from flowers. This kind of belief, of an immediate heavenly reward for those who die during a religious battle, has found its equivalence in all religion's that choose to lull ignorant innocent young boys into a religious battle, where they are promised immediate transport to some god's heaven, if they should loose their life while fighting the unholy holy battle.

In more recent historical time, we see the power of a religion to call forth multitudes of people to make religious battles for the conquest of lands, to acquire booty, and to establish religious domination or religious conversion over the peoples whose lands they occupy by means of their powerful military presence. In these historic times, whole empires rose and fell on the tides of the multitudes of believers, who willingly bowed down in worship of the most simple-minded religious doctrines. Here we see the waves of religiously inspired conquests wash back and forth across a continent, leaving as each tide recedes, a havoc of human suffering and death, only to be washed over by yet another opposing wave of useless religiously inspired conquest. In the battles that religions have repeatedly waged against one another, nothing of value has ever, not even in one instance, been established. They have all been a dance of insane madness, where pain and terrible sufferings were their only sustaining music, it has all been a horrible dissonant melody too shameful to recount. Yet to this day ignorant fools with contagious poisoned minds, still sing praises to the glory of it all, a glory that never, ever, existed. If instead, we sang of the truth of it all, then possibly we would become so disgusted and ashamed with the ugliness of the song that we would wish it forever forgotten, and never mentioned again.

But even in today's world, religions forever dwell on and encourage us to memorialize forever some of the most terrible and unholy memories from their tragic and fear filled past. They delight in encouraging us to relive ancient past fears by ritualizing them and forever presenting them to us as some sacred holy pageant. Gruesome ritual religious pageants, where the primary images and symbols of human torture and death are carried about, and sadly, the pageant's religious minded observers see these objects not as what in reality they are, but instead, because they have been made blind to truth, they see them as inspiring holy images. Some of today's religion's find the need to more fully dramatize their dogma's purported past holy pain and sufferings, and their ritual pageants involve the ritualized self beating of one's body until blood freely flows or other methods of real life sacrificial blood letting by means specifically indicated in their unholy holy books.

Even though in today's world where religions in their weakened state have in most cases lost the power to physically torture and murder the population, there are some places within the world where a single religion is still the absolute dominant legal and moral authority. Some of today's religions are still able to resort to inhuman tortures, murder, and other physical and mental means to control their populations. When religions have either the protection of a sovereign state, or when in some cases, the religion itself is in control of the sovereign state, then in those cases the dominant religion finds itself free to impose whatever fears and/or tortures and penalties on the population, which they believe are appropriate to strictly enforce their old unholy holy dogmatic doctrines. It is usual in such cases, where the religious fundamentalists have control of both the primary unholy holy books of the faith, and to the detriment of their followers, they also have complete control over the interpretations of those works, that the most evil of persecutions are born into existence. From such a situation, of complete power and control, inevitably arises interpretations of the basic religious doctrines that are beyond any direct correspondence to the original dogma and are without any authoritative grounds on which interpretations can be reasonably based. From such situations in today's world we have the evidence provided from some areas of the world, where whole populations of some countries are so subservient to the authorities of the controlling dominant religion, the populations are little better off than are out-and-out thought slaves. In these countries the population's hopes have been replaced by fear, their dreams have been replaced with nightmares, their yearnings for a better future for themselves and their families have been replaced with a sinister resolve that their future will be worse than today. The saddest part of their tragic story is, the population always seems to be befuddled as to how such a terrible situation could ever fall upon them from their holy religion, whose tenets are all about, loving, caring, helping, forgiving, respecting and believing in the goodness of their god. The population can never quite understand how such good tenets can be twisted from their base into, hating, uncaring, obstructing, vengeance, torture, or murder, and yet still be tied to the goodness of their god.

Today, Religions in most parts of the world are no longer able to frighten the population with their unholy condemnation of those persons whose beliefs are different from theirs. They are no longer able to drag human sacrificial victims to their god's temples and there sacrifice their life to the religion's unidentifiable god. They are no longer able to tear apart a living person's body that has been tied to a mechanical racking device. They are no longer able to burn at the stake those persons who oppose their religious ideas. They are no longer able to hide their inhuman crimes of horrible torture and death in dark castle or temple caverns. They are generally no longer able to call vast ignorant multitudes into purposeless religious conflicts. We must with the most seriousness, ask ourselves why is it that religions no longer generally engage in these activities as a means of demonstrating their divinely given power over us mere human subjects? We must ask, is it because religions have willingly changed their modus operandi? No, no, and no, is the truthful answer. They, the religions have not changed by their own volition; they have been forced to change, because an enlightened general population simply will no longer put up with the religion's sacrificial extravagances of the past. Now days religions are bound, by what a more or less enlighten population will allow, and in this way, and by this means alone, religion's once omnipotent power has been reduce merely to their threatening screams about sending us off to their imaginary hell where they claim we will be mercilessly tortured for eternity. What kind of fool would ever offer up their allegiance to such a monstrous unkind philosophy, a philosophy whose most prolific monuments have always been cemeteries, where lie the multitudes of dead corpses who silently testify to the truth or falsehood of it all. And it has always been the case that when religions have been caught red-handed dancing in the arms of their evil devil, they claim it was actually someone else.

THE TRAP AT OUR FEET

In the United States the people's constitution forbids government from furthering the cause of any religion or from inhibiting any religion's right to freely exercise, within the religion, their religious tenets. But the members of the United States government openly and shamelessly ignore their constitutionally defined responsibilities in this matter, and they openly support religions by allowing them to be, so-called, non-profit organizations, which are free from taxation. If this governmental relief from taxes is not in fact a direct governmental support of religion, then there must be some great misunderstanding by the common taxable people of what "support" means. And in this clearly, yet unspoken, direct support of religion by the government, the common people independent of their affiliation with any religion are forced by the government's taxation of the people to make up the difference of the unbelievably vast amounts of tax monies that should by every right have been paid into the government's treasuries by those religions that suck up vast sums of monies from their religious followers, the followers who first pay it into their temple's untouchable treasuries, and then those same followers, those same people are allowed to deduct their payments to religion from their own personal or corporate taxes, all of which leaves a most gigantic hole in the federal and state treasuries, and the tax paying citizens are financially squeezed into making up the loss. Then after all this monetary hurt has been compounded and absorbed by the overly taxed population, the religions, do something that is not exactly to be found in any of their basic doctrines. They take some of the vast monies from their temple treasuries and they buy, the complete or partial ownership of radio and television stations, newspapers, magazines, publishing companies, book publishers, automobile manufactures and retail dealerships. They buy up huge tracts of land, and they invest their temple's monies in every corner of the supposedly free economy, and there they accumulate an enormous secret financial empire, whose many economic parts are beholden to religion's ever growing power hungry whims. From religion's secret powerful financial earthly empires, they cast their unholy holy shadows across the government and the regulations and laws of the nation, from which they are able to gain by means of their monetary force of persuasion, laws and regulations that are evermore favorable to their every means of increasing their economic power. It's a nasty, dirty, and well established cycle, where escape from taxation eventually gives rise to a powerful economic religious monster, which is free to grow without any kind of effective restraint, a condition that if left uncontrolled will finally leave all of the economic chips in religion's power-greedy hands, and which will inevitably bring a surprised population into bowing down to whatever trivial or monumental desires religion wants them to fulfill.

You frequently hear persons of some religious persuasion parroting over-and-over again that the United States of America's success is because the country was founded upon sound religious doctrines including a belief in some un-described invisible god, but the real story, the real truth, is that the foundations of our nation are sunken deeply in the rocks of commerce and social compromise which have been and are the primary substances of their anchorage. And our nation's growth, survival, and successes have come in spite of religious doctrines, not because of them. Within our young and growing country, while one religious faction was forbidding something in one section of the country, a different religious faction was performing it in a distant part of the country. When some religious group in the south forbids dancing, some other group in the north began dancing up a storm. If some religious group forbids alcoholic beverages, others were toasting to their demise. When some religious group forbids making so-called graven images, then some other group begins whittling at making statues. When one religious group was forbidding the eating of pork, another religious group was hosting a pork barbeque. When one religious group forbids the use of automobiles, a different group was using them to speed into the future. When one religious group forbids masturbation, a whole nation is enjoying its pleasures. When one religious group forbids measures for birth control, others are enjoying sex without the worries associated with conception. Our nation's successes have been primarily because no one religious faction has ever been strong enough to dominate the thinking of the entire nation. Our nation's great successes have come into existence, primarily because there are so many individually fragmented religions within the nation, and none of them have, so far, been able to completely dominate our government and our other institutions, although their unholy dream is to eventually gain that domination. Yes, surely the historical evidence from across the nation shows, it is not because of religion, that we are a great nation, but it is instead, in spite of religion.

It is the fundamental nature of a civilized society to encourage and persuade its members to exhibit a moral behavior. Religions propagandize that they are the source of society's moral beliefs, but the moral beliefs, which are of the greatest meaningful value to our kind, were all originated in the very distant past by the peoples of a time, who were becoming evermore civilized and less savage than was their ancestors. The best moral values of any and every modern society are common to all civilized societies of the world, and they are without any ties to the claimed divine sources of any particular religion, they are common, independent of the ambient religion, because they are beliefs which are common to our natural evolving and evermore civilized outlook upon the world and our own nature. Many of the outdated beliefs which religions still today declare as rules for moral conduct have long been bankrupt, and they are of no value to any society which necessarily must evolve and change with the passage of time and the ever-better understanding of our own true nature, and of the universe which surrounds us.

Even in some areas of United States of America, where by covenants of the people's constitution, the separation of church and state is supposed to be respected and protected, there are some areas of our country where religions dominate and essentially control the local governments, and where the governments due the bidding on behalf of, and for, the religious authorities. In some of these places the local police are little more than a religious bowing Gestapo, which by means of written law, or by the more hidden means of extreme intimidation, lies, theft, the planting of false evidence, and the bearing of false witness, they work the will of the religion against any members of the population who openly defy the church's authority, or are seen to be outside of some religious moral boundary. And so we can understand the inevitable sad results of our educational systems in these areas, where the local religion or religions have so infiltrated within the educational system that the so-called educated population, allows, with an unthinking and uncaring acceptance, the defilement of the United States constitution's intent, and the shabby treatment of those citizens who do not live up to the doctrinal standards of the controlling religion. In these areas, there exists only the barest pretence of a government that might be called democratic; the government and other institutions in these areas are found, by any kind of reasonable inspection, to be out-and-out religious theocracies. There is no need to name by state or local where these full-blown and half-blown religious theocracies thrive, they are all well known by most persons, persons who are unwilling to point the finger and speak out. Why are we concerned about converting a foreign tyrannical government into to a democratic government, we should first in our home country see that the constitution is respected, and that all localities are free to establish a democratic style of government and get religion back to were it belongs, out of education, out of government, out of police forces, out of the judiciary, out of the victimless laws written in our law books, out of the laws that were instigated by belief in some out-of-date ignorant two thousand year old outlook on life. Religions need to be forced to crawl back into their own dark religious shell, and their again become what they purport themselves to be, and to stop slowly and stealthy creeping into every aspect of a society wherein lies religion's hopes for some future complete domination of the society. Let religions do whatever rituals they want to do, or believe they need to do, within their churches, shrines, and temples, but keep their unholy blood stained ignorant hands off from attempting to control every aspect of society. We have in today's world clearly seen all of the evidence that we should ever need to see of what inevitably happens whenever religions are free to have their way.

We have some little bit of luck in the common people's growing doubts about religiously accepting some doctrines, which beg from the point of view of the holy sanctity of life, when in fact their arguments are little more than a weak disguise of religion's desire to have, regardless of any cost to families or to society, an endless supply of evermore-and-more babies, who are then available to be brainwashed into religion's marching army of those who willingly perpetuate their outdated doctrines by means of their contagious poisoned minds. Today's religions callout to their members to abstain from any sexual relationships that do not produce children, and to abstain from using any kind of device that can stop the sex act's fertilization of the human egg. But we can see that most sensible, people who are still able to think for themselves and make decisions for their own and for their family's best interest, ignore these religious declarations to embrace their several thousand year old and grossly out-dated moralities, and to go about their lives as is best for them, and not for what is best for maintaining the power basis of their ever power hungry religion.

Today, to the call from the various right-wing religious fundamentalists, for armies of their believers to come forth and fight for their ridiculous unbelievable doctrines, and whose banners of battle are waved by simple minded persons who have been made blind to truth by their poisoned contagious minds, their battle calls are ineffectual, and their power in today's world is shown to be trivial, almost nothing, as compared to the great numbers who could be called forth to do battle by their more ancient and much more powerful religious predecessors.

There is a test that can discover if a religion has already enough power to begin closing its lethal grip upon a society; that test is—if—or if not an individual is able to publicly question a religion's motivations and the truth of its religious doctrines. If this can be done without any official threatening to the individual, then religion has not yet weaseled its way into controlling all of the power points within a society, and then a society still has at least a small window of opportunity for placing strict bounds upon religion's ever growing hunger for more and more power. In a sane society we refuse to allow a single business or group of united businesses to dominate all of an entire commerce, we impose regulations to keep them in their proper place and in a proper perspective to the overall economy. We must be wise enough to place the same kinds of limiting bounds on where and how religions are allowed to operate, and this would be to the benefit to our nation and to the world. We can clearly see the results where religion has grown out of control, and by its domination, brings danger and fear to those who are of a different idea.

THIS PAGE IS THE SACRED SEAL
OF THE RELIGION OF THE FUTURE

THOSE WHO WILLINGLY PROCEED
PAST THIS SEAL OF TIME ARE FOR-
BIDDEN TO RETURN TO THEIR
WORLD UNCHANGED BY THAT
WHICH IS HERE RECORDED

THE CALL TO JOIN THE FUTURE

If any merciless devil exists in some hidden crevice of eternal darkness, then he, yes he, is and has been the god of the world's religions and has led them from the darkest ignorant retched unholy past, through history's painful and bloody journey where today still steeped in their same old out of date ignorance, they claim to have every answer, to every question ever asked, but by their own long history they have demonstrated, they have no answers, none at all, and they have embarrassedly shown, not only, that they do not have any answers, none whatsoever, but they don't even know the correct questions. We the people have paid in full, with our coins of pain, hunger, fear, sorrow and death, the price that was demanded for our misplaced faith, for our own ignorant alliances with the disguised creatures of hell. This evilest of philosophies never came forth showing its true monstrous image, it came upon us disguised as a gentle lamb of light and goodness. But now our debt, our ignorance is finally finished, and we bow to ignorance— no more. Our hope is now to search, to understand, and to find our God within the nature of God's creation, where is to be found the only clues to what is right or wrong, to truth and falsehood, and where we can discover some hopeful means of salvation from hard times, and from personal death.

Our journey through life is a story, our story, and our story is a part of the overall story of our kind's time in history. We are fed-up with dying and not ever knowing how the rest of the story comes out, we have made our contributions to future history, and we want to know how the story that becomes the future turns out. We want to work towards each of us being able to experience evermore of the future story of our kind.

An important part of our challenge is to develop a guiding philosophy, a true religion, that can lead us safely and successfully into the future. We can no longer afford for events to fall unexpectedly upon an ignorant humankind. It is the very basic nature of nature itself, that for every species there is a test for survival that is ever greater and more challenging than the last test, which they survived.

We should clearly understand there are going to be unexpected challenges from nature, and humankind can no longer afford the added burden of an archaic hatred between nations, religions, races, and other differences that are of no realistic consequence whatsoever to our kind. We live in most precarious time, when the power of even a small group could rain havoc upon the heads of vast numbers of our people. It is totally unacceptable that an uneducated society should rises up in any way against what is truly our own kind. We are now in great need to be united to face and solve the problems of our world for the betterment of all that are upon this world.

We, none of us, can any longer afford to go forth each day and see before us only the small narrow world of our own daily existence. We must, each of us, put aside our prejudices of yesterday. We must use our best intellect to see this world as a place that is home to the greatest dreams and the greatest creature that the God of the Universe has here created. We must understand that we are completely responsible for our destiny, and the destiny of all that is around us, and we must realize this fact in its fullness. We have a holy obligation to all of life, that life itself, must realize the best that it can dream.

We are at a time when for the best of all reasons, we need all, and that means all, of our people to be united in an understanding of our need to strive together, to build the best of all possible worlds, and an ever better educated, tolerant, and understanding population.

We need the best of all to come forward and to join in a solemn bond to design, make, and implement a new and good philosophy that will with understanding and humility lead us with dignity and our best hopes to a future of greater learning, and to the goodness of all we can dream.

If you as an individual hope that you can find some personal philosophy of life that intrinsically gives your life both value and continuing hope for an always better tomorrow, then it is for you I have written this book. I write in the belief that most person's dreams have strong and common bonds, and there are multitudes of people in the world who are waiting to join in a solemn communion, a communion of positive purpose, of good intent, and one that transcends all of the old historic barriers and ancient taboos.

We should be overly tired of those who have been seriously and religiously brain-washed, and have forever been screaming out "We should not be playing god and experimenting with the secretes of life and death." But as usual, they are wrong, wrong, and wrong, for that is exactly what we should be doing, if we are to ever find a pathway to an ever-better future for our kind, and for life in general.

We are not just Pavlov's dogs reincarnated; we are not the animal who acts out a task for just a sugar cube's sweet positive reward. We are the ones who willingly take on tasks of bitter taste, tasks that have no sweet enjoyment to consume, but we willingly do it, with a hope that in the future someone else may taste a sweeter time.

We are the mortals, whose potential destiny after a long gestation within the cocoon atmosphere of Earth can bloom forth as a new immortal creature, which flies fearlessly in to the heavens and on into the eternal depths of space.

THE SONG OF FATE

Fate is a song that begins, so delicate, so distant, it cannot be heard. Like some calm that will be the wind, gently comes its melody to caress the fabric of time. And whose final beat—is reality—solid—and true.

THE NEW BEGINNING

THE RELIGION OF THE FUTURE

(GENESIS)

In the beginning there was Hell. Turmoil was upon the face of the deep. Light and Darkness had no meaning. All is God and God is All. God's music of purpose is bound within the body of the elements, and it dances hidden even in this deepest of chaotic hells. All is God and God is All. The secret song of purpose was in the beginning only a dream, a dream nearly smothered in the churning oblivion of chaotic matter, time, and space. All is God and God is All. Through eons of time's separating, settling, and metamorphosing, form appeared as hope and the dream of all dreams began its slow seep from things and places hidden in the deep. All is God and God is All. For eons unmeasured, fate's distant melody of natural magic, too faint to have a place, gains strength to show some sign of its holy face. All is God and God is All. Elemental things kiss and dance in every way entwined, and they make a tune whose harmony is more and deeper than the soul of humankind. All is God and God is All. A kind of music that adds on to itself, and becomes stronger and richer, growing slowly, but without end. A music that in time will define the cricket's chirp and how the willow will bend. All is God and God is All. The elements drift and flow within the streams of time, and make one-and-one more than two, to define the molds and slime. All is God and God is All. What was just a feeble song sifting through the new dawn will with patient waiting become a symphony of light. A romance of tones so strong it separates day and night. All is God and God is All. It's harmony so sweet and true, it penetrates every crack, and sets to motion shapes and forms that no force of chaos can turn back. All is God and God is All. The music is little eyes that look up to behold the starry sky. It's little feet that tramp the Earth, and creatures that can almost fly. All is God and God is All. The music fluxes and dances in every ocean's tide. It flows with streams and rivers down every mountainside. Sometimes it thunders in the drums of a monster's steps. Sometimes an opera of screams it plays across the land, but every note, of every song, was written by divine command All is God and God is All. This wonderful symphony, grows and grows. At times sweet melodies conjure up a slight dissonance, giving contrast its time and place. A music so complex, it defines every feather, and every face. All is God and God is All. A God's many eyes open from being long blind, and see God's holy body stretching out from the center of the creatures of every kind. All is God and God is All. The great master divine symphony ever becoming more than before, strives for the time when nature will stand up, and sing its part of the score. All is God and God is All. A time when the words of the song are at first unclear. A time when each trial song brings not but pain to each hearing ear. All is God and God is All. This opera of hope and fear moans from the throats of ignorant things that swing in trees or live beneath the ground. It is a gruesome song of trials and sufferings that struggle for some meaning to be found. All is God and God is All. Sweet and sour music of the all, your time has come for sounds of substance and meaning within each creature's call. All is God and God is All. Great, oh how great, this harmony of songs and rhythms in ever style. Its power and drive resonates within the heart of everything, of every kind. It echoes and resonates from every creature's mind. All is God and God is All. An echo that reflects more and more truly every little piece of nature's song, which new senses let through. An echo named intelligence within each creature grew. All is God and God is All. Long struggling to understand it all, each creature made every mistake, every miscall. All is God and God is All. Within the sad wanderings of time itself, long eons stretched toward a future, where blind and dumb prophets named the past, and told of what would come. But, they were always wrong. It was an understandable mistake, for they never really heard God's song. All is God and God is All. A song that throbbed and pulsed from every, everything. But a song not in the words of any nation's king. All is God and God is All. A song with a harmony that resonates from each stone, each star, each life, and echoes in every mind. It's a song that's in one language common to us all. It is the language of the God, who is the All of All. All is God and God is All. No Urim and Thummim is needed to understand God's words, they are in common language, common to us all. And, that language is, simply nature's all. All is God and God is All. Anyone, from any place or time, is free to understand it clearly, and its wondrous depth sublime. All is God and God is All. It's glorious truths cannot be summed up in any foolish books. Such writings are filled with hidden poisonous hooks. All is God and God is All. Such a song of complicated and wondrous weavings, takes just work to sift it out. It gives up its holy meanings only to those of intelligence, those who are mentally stout. All is God and God is All. Those who yearn to know and to understand must undertake a journey of discovery and learning, a laborious search, and they shall be rewarded to see it all, from a high and godly perch. All is God and God is All

THE FOREVER DREAM

(EXODUS)

I say to you the peoples of my new tribe, oh you sad mortals, you seekers, searchers, and dreamers. You, who are longing to know, yearning to love, hoping to be forever. You, who have crept forward in time against the most impossible odds, struggled, and survived against every insult. Your example of tenaciousness is the central kernel, the holy banner of your kind's substance. You, who are believing, hoping, dreaming of time without end. You, whose hope of eternal tomorrows, finally knocks hard against the door of ultimate ends. You, whose toil is to open that door, have dreamt the magical dream, the most powerful dream, the dream that dreams itself onward from present time, to the future where lies the land of new frontiers.

I say unto the nations and their churches, why have you bound the minds of my children with superstitions and ignorance and chained them from discovering the wondrous and marvelous details of my ever-continuing creation. Why have you bound them and forcefully tied them with awkward customs that should have died a thousand years ago. It is from your own love of power and your fear that they will see your true ignorance, which is in its full bloom, that you have done these things. You have held my children dumb like the unthinking beast and caused them to continue to suffer ancient ills that civilized peoples should have long ago conquered. You have carried forth the ghosts and monsters of the darkest past in your company and forced them into the minds of my children, so that my children suffer needlessly from ancient fears that should have long been dead and finished.

I say unto the nations and their churches, you, the worst of all things, have prepared my children for the tomb instead of for life. You have pulled the black veil across their minds and blinded them from discovering those most powerful things, which reside within the marvels of my creation. You have clothed the sickness of your true spirit, your utter weakness, your ignorance, and your hypocrisy with the cloth of bright words of love, kindness, and truth, but the real naked truth of you shows from behind all of those fine garments, it is revealed in the ways you have held my peoples, my children, in dirt and ignorance. I say unto you, who are the most vial of all self fabricated creatures, and to your mindless flocks of unthinking followers, and to your great ignorance, that your time of power is come to its end, and my peoples will soon point to the past where your deeds are clearly written and they will loath you forever for the disease of your ignorance, which you have succored and nurtured in the guise of unchanging truth. I shall guide my peoples, my new tribe, in an exodus from the twisted illogical nightmare you have woven, as does a spider weave its trap, and you have wrapped your horrible nightmare around my people's intellect, and I shall lead the people of my new tribe into a better place, where the future is eternal hope, and where their land will be filled with goodness and the true joys and hopes of life.

I say to my the peoples of my new tribe, within your world there are many possible directions that you might take to escape from the land of confinements imposed by the ancient illogical taboos. The direction, which I here pointed you to, is the direction of sure hope. If you are wise enough to choose my direction, and it is your choice, because I have from your beginnings given you the option of always deciding your own destiny. So be now mature and wise in your choice, and then your future can be the best you can dream, and when that dream has been fulfilled, then you can dream a newer dream, a fresh dream of another world that is then the best you can dream. And in this manner will your future, and the future of all of your children, always be the very best you can imagine, the best you can dream. Surely you can understand which direction is the best for you, for those you love, for your children, and for your children's children into the future; therefore you must either choose to make your exodus from the illogical restraints spewed up by the ignorance of the dark past, or to continue into the future in the same manner as is pointed to by the unholy historical evidence of your past.

And I say to the peoples of my new tribe, when some of your kind were forcefully driven from the gardens, those most ancient landscapes of your kind's origins, they were driven to leave, not by hunger, but instead by the separation of their ideas from the common ideas held by the others who occupied the gardens. Outside of the gardens, outside of their beloved home was the landscape of a physical world undiscovered by their kind, a world where there was great uncertainty about their future survival, a world of ever-new obstacles and tests that my Mother Nature had blindly laid as deathtraps for all those who by their physical and mental struggling could not surmount those snags. It was to be, that surely only those who were the strongest of mind left their known home, the home of their birth and the home of their young beginnings. This has always the case, but you can see there are a few of my children, who are willing to endure the hardships and dangers, which always lie hidden within the folds of unfolding new frontiers. You, my peoples, have inevitably arrived at the time, when you have conquered all of the geographical frontiers of the world, and you can call any of them, your home. But, I say unto you, there has always been another frontier before you, which you have never been successful at seeing clearly, and that is the frontier of time, the ultimate frontier of your future, you have never been able to see into that distant landscape. Here you are trapped by the Earth's geological landscape, you have it all—and it has you—it is your trap—and your cage. The nations of people are spread to all the realms of the Earth, and within those nations are the frustrated persons, who know not yet that they belong to my new tribe, and they seek an exodus leading to new adventures, adventures unending that can be found only in the newest frontiers. They are people like you, who would willingly escape to find or make a better life, but they believe there is no place left to go. And I say unto you, the greatest frontier of all is left to be discovered, to be had, but as usual most of your kind cannot see it, and even if they did, they would not be willing to pay the hard price escaping demands. Only the bravest of you, those who can long endure the rigorous nature of logic can go to the new frontiers, but it takes many years of preparation, yet for those who can endure, there are frontiers without any ending. There are frontiers that have no barriers of geology or of international boarders. And I say unto you, the only barriers are from the many of your kind, who are always fearful of new frontiers, fearful of any new future, fearful of any and every change. They are the same kind as those who stayed behind at home in the ancient gardens of your beginnings, where they foolishly believed they were safe from the new future, while the brave and dynamic ones of your kind were searching out new lands and continents. And I say unto you, you the ones of my new tribe, those who are marked, and within themselves know they are marked as the chosen brave creators and discoverers, you will develop the imaginative frontiers of the mind into tomorrow's best realities. And I say unto you, those of my new tribe, those of you who are now already prepared, and those who would study and work to understand nature and its frontiers must in some manner be drawn into common places, or have an ethereal place of common communion. Then you who are the brave and creative ones of your kind, and who are now in a sense trapped by being isolated, will when associated together make magic so great that the air would be filled with excitement about the new possibilities for ever better tomorrows. But, there is not yet established a common place for you to find each other, a place where you can share ideas and work together for creating a much better world. In what few real intellectual sanctuaries of partial freedom are left, you must be always wise enough and strong enough to let the frontiers of the mind, frontiers where the best future lies, grow within your restricted geographical boarders. This is the best hope your kind has now. You must protect your most precious freedoms to create, speak, think, and write, this is all you now have that can save your kind from blind ignorance and from nature's blind disasters and can yet lead your kind to an exodus from the restraining taboos and old unbelievable philosophies and unbelievable doctrines of the past. And I say unto you, prepare the instruments, places, and methods, which will bring you together into the congregation of my new tribe and into a common communion with all of those who use the strength of logical reasoning for our holy purpose.

SAMEID

And alone Sameid came forth out from the Land of Same. And Sameid traveled across and through a dreadful and vast wilderness, where life was a stranger to the landscape. And Sameid saw he was in a land ruled solely by the harshest spirit of the wind. It was an unforgiving land, where hot uncaring winds blew hard and unyielding in their determination to be a curse upon anyone who would dare to set foot upon this, their land, and the wind was a curse even unto any wondering or lost traveler who would try to escape from the wind's land by traveling with great haste through it. The unforgiving and torturous wind parched Sameid's dry and bleeding lips. And Sameid was in great need to ration the water he carried in a leather bottle, a bottle which he had fashioned by his own hands from the skin of a goat, whose flesh he had offered up as a smoldering sacrifice to his invisible god, the god who was the same god for all the people of his tribe of Sameites. And Sameid cried out to his god to provide protection to him from the harsh and merciless hot blowing wind, or to cause the wind to stop of its blowing. But the howling wind smothered Sameid's prayers and pleadings, as if they were just the tiny meowing of an infant kitten, and the wind blew evermore violently, as if the spirit of the wind understood Sameid's pleadings, and was mocking Sameid's feeble efforts.

And it came to pass that eventually Sameid came to a very large stone. And then to gain some easing of his unpleasant situation, Sameid curled his body around the stone that the stone might be between him and the awful cruel wind. But the wind changed its direction and came anew directly at Sameid, then the wind swallowed up the great stone and by using the structures of the stone as its vocal cords, the wind howled out both a warning and a curse. And at hearing the wind speak, a powerful fear came unto Sameid and he quaked with the fear that he might loose his life. And Sameid feared that the wind was a living and seeing thing, an invisible devil that was certain to take his life as an offering to this barren and lifeless wilderness, where no other life was to be found, except for Sameid's fearful being. And Sameid came away from being curled around the great stone and made his way straight and fast that he might possibly escape from this unnatural lifeless place of winds that cared not for any living creature, or for any other living thing. Every small thing in this lifeless land the wind had blown away and the land was barren of all things except nature's hard and substantial rocks.

And it came to pass that Sameid after making a great effort at quickly scurrying straight away in one direction, which was the direction that the wind was blowing towards, that Sameid came to another land where the wind was dead, but where the wind had left monuments sculpted by its once powerful strength, and the dead wind's great monuments stretched to the distant horizon, the monuments were dunes, huge mountainous dunes of sand, dunes made from billions upon billions upon billions of tiny grains of sand, sand that once had a kind of life riding on the back of the now dead, but once living spirit of the wind. And Sameid was sorely discouraged at seeing this vast new wilderness of this land of unmoving and forever-sleeping sand. But then, for each step Sameid tried to take, the sand at his feet became instantly alive, and it flowed itself around his feet, and it tried to bury Sameid's feet within a shallow tomb of sand. Sameid cried out to his god to stop the sand from burying his feet at every step he took. But the sand had no ears with which to hear the commands from Sameid's god, even if any commands were issued, so the sand could not obey orders spoken into the air, and the grains of sand had not their own volition; they were prisoners of their place, and only gravity's structure disturbed could cause them some lifelike movements to make. Sameid struggled at what seemed a never-ending struggle up one side of a great dune of sand, and then his body went tumbling over-and-over-and-over and down the dune's other side. Sameid spoke unkind words about the dunes, but not having ears the dunes were not offended, but the sand dunes even being un-offended were still steadfast at offering a great resistance to Sameid's determined journey. Sameid was discouraged that his progress through this wilderness of sand was bitterly slow. And Sameid was in need of any substance to sustain his life, and so Sameid consumed the last of the water from the goatskin bottle he had fashioned with his own hands. Sameid held his empty bottle up to the sky, and he cried out loudly and pleaded to his god that the goatskin bottle might again be filled with life's sustaining water, but the bottle remained empty.

And on and on Sameid struggled up a dune and down the other side, up another dune, and down the other side. Sameid soon became exhausted, and lacking any water to revitalized his dehydrated body, at the bottom of a giant dune he fainted. Sameid fell down in the sand, and his lips were so parched from being so long dry, that he could not call out to his invisible god, or to any creature for help, that someone might hear his cries and come to his rescue. Sameid thought to himself that his desire, his own secrete dream to seek out and to discover a new land, which was not always the same, had become his own self made nightmare and curse, and his life was surely to come to its final end, here in the sandy armpit of a giant sand dune, which was itself the same as every other dune.

Sameid closed his eyes and accepted what he believed was his inescapable fate, his personal doom. Sameid drifted into a deep, but painless sleep, and there a very strange and different dream began to unfold the tapestry of its sensual images, sounds, and emotions. There came into his dream a sound, a single pleasant tone, but no, it wasn't just a single pleasant tone, it was many different tones one fallowing after another, and the tones lingered within each other's midst, where by their presence together, they formed a melody. And upon hearing the pleasant melody, which was formed from different tones, a tear of divine water formed in the sleeping eye of Sameid, and the tear pooled, and it overflowed and ran slowly down Sameid's check, so beautiful was it to hear for the first time different tones coming sometimes together, and sometimes one after another, instead of just one ever repeated monotonous tone. And Sameid smiled in his deep sleep for he now had heard something that was different instead of what is always the same. And he said unto himself within his dream, that when he returned to the Land of the Sameites, he would tell everyone there of the wondrous pleasing different sounds that he had discovered in the land that he found, but knew not where it was located.

And a person walked into Sameid's dream, and Sameid was alarmed at seeing this stranger within his dream, for the stranger was clothed as Sameid had never before seen, the stranger's clothes were completely different than Sameid had ever seen in his homeland of the Sameites, where his people were all dressed exactly, precisely, the same as every other Sameite and without any, even the slightest, variation whatsoever in their form of dress. And Sameid spoke to the stranger in his dream, and he said unto the stranger that the stranger looked very unusual and peculiar in his style of clothing. And the stranger replied that his style was intended to be different from the manner in which another individual was dressed. And Sameid asked how that could be possible, and speculated that such independence of clothing styles would cause people to become un-groupable and then people would be left as if sanding alone, to be alone and separate from all others. But the stranger in Sameid's dream replied, that his people are all different by their own nature, with, or without clothes, they are each one of them different, one from any other, and that no common clothing can make the same out of that which is not in its first instance the same, but is in its first instance different. And Sameid was amazed by what the stranger in the dream had said, and Sameid was skeptical about the truth of this pronouncement. Sameid said unto the stranger within his dream, you are only one, what evidence is there that what you say might possibly be true? And the stranger in Sameid's dream turned and beckoned to those who were in the outskirts of the dream, that they might come foreword into the revealing light of the dream, and there to become themselves evidence of what the stranger had spoken. And Sameid beheld a multitude of people came into the light of his dream, and he was amazed beyond any previous amazement by what he saw revealed unto his dream's eyes. Each and every person of the multitude was either in their manner of dress or by some other means different from every, and any other one of them. And Sameid asked to the stranger, but how can any of you be classified as the same as another, so that you might be prejudged by seeing you common marks of classification. And the stranger answered, their are no marks of any kind that you can make upon any person, which makes them the same as any other person, because its is under any showing signs that the individual in truth resides, and there are no marks of clothing, color, or of any other kind which can make us the same, for we are not in the first place the same, in our first instance we are not the same, but are each one of us different, and to be seen as different, in our form of dressing, or any other difference, is only the truth of the individual which lies beneath it all. And Sameid looked at each person within the multitude, and as he looked, Sameid heard the tones from the first part of his dream, and he understood that the different tones where the cause of the beautiful melody, and though different, the beauty of the melody could not exist without those individual differences. And so, as Sameid look at the multitudes, he saw they were also a kind of a most beautiful visual melody, and he then understood the meaning of his dream, and he awakened to discovered that the stranger within his dream had filled full Sameid's goat skin water bottle, and Sameid after taking a drink of the refreshing liquid of life, excitedly began his journey back to the Land of Same, where he would tell his people of his wonderful visionary insights.

TRIBID

And alone Tribid came out from the Land of Tribulation. For the hardest of cruel times had settled like some fearsome curse across the Land of Tribulation, and in the land every nourishing substance became the diet of crawling and hopping things, or else became grotesquely withered without reason, making them all undesirable for consumption by any but the foulest of lowly creatures. Though thin and weak of body, Tribid was determined and strong of mind to journey out into the vastness of unknown lands. And for his journey Tribid had fashioned a leather purse from the skin of a she-goat, whose skinny few bits of flesh he had offered up as a sacrifice to his invisible god, but before he had made his sacrificial offering, he snatched a few pieces of the she-goat's flesh that he might dry it and later he put the dried flesh it into the purse he had made by his own hands from the she-goat's hide. And thus prepared, and with the blessings from the priests of his invisible god, and with his leather purse stuffed with dried flesh, Tribid set out upon his journey to seek out and find some powerful magic which he might bring back home to his land.

And by the power of that yet unknown magic Tribid hoped to lift the curse, which had settled its invisible carcass across his beloved land of Tribulation. With the greatest of determination Tribid went forth into the unknown territories of unknown lands, and as he journeyed he wandered into a land where the ground was covered by rounded boulders of rock. The rocks were of every size from the smallest of pebbles to huge round boulders the size of a man's house. And this place of rounded rocks was most difficult for Tribid to journey across. Like traps laid out by an evil giant, the rocks and boulders though not alive, twisted Tribid's feet and bumped his shins against their hardness, and they cared not about continually hurting and bruising Tribid's frail body. And Tribid struggled on through this hurtful Land of Boulders, and to bolster his determination, he thought of the magic he might discover at the end of his quest. After much walking, stumbling, and bumping, Tribid was tired and hungry, and he sat down upon a boulder the size of a chair, and there on the boulder he rested and took from his leather purse a piece of the dried she-goat's flesh, which he chewed upon for nourishment, and while resting and eating he look out across the wilderness of great boulders. In every direction, for as far as Tribid could see, there were heaps of boulders of every size from small pebbles to rocks as large as a man's house. And seeing how vast was the Land of Boulders and already having known of their hurt and the great difficulty of traveling through this land, Tribid called out to his invisible god to clear a path for him that it might easy his crossing through this most difficult rocky landscape. But Tribid's invisible god was maybe busy with his own concerns, and maybe hadn't noticed Tribid's miserable predicament, for no help came to easy Tribid's journey, and the boulders all sat, just were they had always been sitting.

Discourage but not without hope, Tribid stood up from the rock on which he had been resting and he continued on with his painful journey through the Land of Boulders, but finally from hurt and shear exhaustion Tribid again was overcome by weakness and he again stopped and sat upon a boulder to rest. Tribid took the last piece of dried she-goat's flesh from his leather purse, and he chewed upon the dried flesh that it might give him the strength of body and of mind to continue on with his journey. And as Tribid rested he looked up into the sky, and he saw a black raven flying, and in the raven's beak was a cluster of grapes, they were very plump grapes, and not withered or shrunken, but delightfully plump, and the cluster of grapes were a delicious sight to behold. Tribid's mouth began to water for in his imagination he could already taste those plump and delicious grapes. And Tribid could see that the course of the black raven's flight was to be straight over his head, and Tribid pleaded with his invisible god that when the raven passed overhead, his god would cause the raven to drop the cluster of plump grapes, or if not the whole cluster, that a few of those delicious grapes might fall free from the cluster, so that Tribid might catch them in his mouth. But as the raven passed over Tribid's head something did fall from the raven, but it was not the cluster of grapes, or even a single grape, but instead one of those droppings that ravens are so fond of using as a salute to those who are below.

Tribid was sorely discouraged, but he had noticed where the straight line of the raven's flight pointed, and although weak and tired and with his leather purse completely empty, Tribid started out in the direction from which the raven had come, and in his mind's eye he visualized delicious grapes, un-withered grapes, large plump grapes, and the power of his vision gave strength to his feet and legs and he hurried, as best he could, stumbling and crawling forward in a straight line through the Land of Boulders. Finally to his eye's amazement from the height of a great boulder, Tribid saw that the Land of Boulders came to its end, and beyond the last few boulders, Tribid saw vast fields of green growth, and rows upon rows of grapevines that were heavy weighed down by great clusters of plump ripe grapes, and he saw fields of huge melons, and as he hurried to reach this land were every kind of delicious thing was flourishing and not being consumed by multitudes of things that hopped or crawled, and where there was a vast bounty of nature's good foods, and that great bounty was greater than he had ever imagined was possible, and even greater than anything he could have dreamed existed.

And Tribid was filled with the joy of his discovery, and he hurried from the last of the Land of Boulders and into the green fields, which were so bountifully plentiful with good things to eat. And Tribid was for a moment fearful, because he thought maybe he had fallen asleep in the Land of Boulders and all of this was only a dream, and to be certain that he was really awake, Tribid pinched himself several times very severally, and each time he pinched, he said ouch! And he was then sure that this land, this agricultural heaven was a thing of reality, and he was certain that some very powerful magic lay upon this land and blessed it with an abundance which overflowed into its every part.

Tribid hurried straight away to the grapevines, and he sat down among the vines with their clusters of grapes, and he began eating the grapes, they were the sweetest, plumpest, and most delicious grapes that Tribid had ever seen, tasted, or eaten. But while Tribid was eating and not paying attention to what was around, a man came through the green fields and came up to Tribid, who was stuffing his mouth full of the grapes, and the man ask Tribid where he was from, since Tribid's costume seemed to be of a style out of a time very long past. And Tribid replied that he had journeyed here from his Land of Tribulation, and he mentioned that he was famished and in need of immediate nourishment, and that is why he was eating the grapes. And the man said the grapes were abundant and Tribid could have all that he desired. Tribid was then quick to fill his leather purse full of the delicious grapes, and he was also anxious to learn of the magical means that made this land so prosperous and rich in all manner of good foods. And Tribid told the man of the great problems, which were always rampant in his Land of Tribulation, and he begged of the man to tell him the name of the magic, which made this land so different from his own Land of Tribulation. And the man felt sympathy for Tribid and for the Land of Tribulation, and so he told to Tribid the names of the magic whose power made this land so bountiful and so different from Tribid's land. And the man bent down low to Tribid, who was still sitting upon the ground, and he whispered into Tribid's ear the names of the secret magic, and the whispered names echoed in Tribid's mind that he might remember them forever and ever and take the names back to his people in the Land of Tribulation. And the two magical names that echoed in Tribid's mind where very strange names to Tribid, and the names were "Chemistry" and "Biology." And Tribid said the magical names over-and-over as he journeyed back through the Land of Boulders to the Land of Tribulation where he would triumphantly deliver the magical names to his people.

DEE NIGHID

And it came to pass that within the Land of Denial that there was born unto the family of Nighid, their first, and what was to be their only child, a beautiful young daughter, who was upon the day of her birth, named Dee. And it was immediately after the girl child's birth, that the priests of the people's invisible god preformed their religious rituals the magical ceremonies, which are prescribed within their holy book for the naming of a girl child, and for bringing the girl child into the flock belonging to their invisible god.

And it was to be seen that Dee, even during her earliest childhood years, was exceptionally enthusiastic about life, always inquisitive and somehow ever prone to questioning those particular and peculiar things, which the religion's taboos declared as, "out of bounds."

And it came to pass that as Dee, year by year grew a bit older and wiser, she formed a strong and powerful interest in seeking to understand something of the nature of all living creatures. And by the time Dee came unto her age of maturity, she had learned to somewhat understand and to sympathize with the trials and tribulations of all of nature's creatures. And Dee came to be known among her own peoples as a person of great compassion and a person of strong and good character, but she was also known by some, as one, who too often asked what was not to be asked, and to sometimes say, what was not to ever be said. But even so, time's eventual ripening opened fully the blossom of her yearnings and there to reveal her spirit's strong predispositions that would direct her by an unseen hand to begin her life's new journey.

And it was to be that by-and-by Dee became irresistibly drawn into becoming an assisting attendant at her people's Infirmary of Divine Mercy. Each and every day, except of course for the day of the holy Sabbath, Dee assisted the powerful priests at the Infirmary of Divine Mercy as they went about their most holy business of laying their heavy hands infused with divine healing upon the feverish heads of the sick and dying, who had been brought there that they might, as willed by their invisible god, either survive their wounds, sores, or illness, or else pass from this life on to that other and better place, where pain and suffering was said to be unknown.

And it came to be, as inevitable time and its ever unfolding events marched solemnly past Dee's inquisitive eyes, she came to see not just the ritual of the intended holy healing, but to also see beyond the rituals, the laying on of the hands, the sprinkling of holy water, or the most powerful ritual of the sprinkling of sacrificial blood upon the patient, and she clearly recognized some things unseen by others. And it came to her as a revealing vision of her divine intellect, that those patients who by the nature of their ailment, would recover from their malady, and those others who would succumb to their malady and die, or be forever maimed, where all determined by the nature of their ailment, independent of whatever holy ritual or prayers were performed by the priests in their behalf.

And Dee became aware that there were those patients who were in need of some powerful intervention beyond mere holy rituals and prayers. And it came to pass that one-day when Dee was performing her duties of assistance, the patient complained to her of a great and unbearable pain within his abdomen, and Dee felt that the patient was hot with fever. And while the priest was performing the sacred healing prayers and rituals over the patient, Dee said unto the priest, we have seen this condition many times before in other patients and in every case the patient has succumbed. And she suggested that maybe the patient's abdomen should be opened up that his ailment's cause might possibly be discovered. And the priest was emotionally shaken by Dee's spoken blasphemy, which was contrary to the words of the holy book, wherein the opening up of a living human body is strictly forbidden. And the priest strongly denied that any discovery of merit could possibly be made by any method forbidden by the holy writings. And so Dee being most strongly rebuked for her suggestion, became silent, and soon the patient died, even though his lifeless body was yet damp with the ritual's sacred holy water.

And it came to pass at another time, there was a young patient who had been severely wounded upon his upper arm, and Dee, from her experience and from her visionary insight, was certain this young man would succumb from his extreme loss of blood which pulsed from the gapping open wound. And Dee quietly watched as the attending high priest wrapped pages of paper from the holy book around and about the bleeding wound and while the high priest tied the holy book's pages firmly in place, he offered up a prayer to the invisible god to spare this man's life, for the man had always been a true and faithful follower of the invisible god's holy book's teachings. And Dee looked upon the bleeding man and she beheld that his body's color was ashen, and she said unto the attending high priest, that the man would surely die from his great loss of blood. And then unable to contain the insight from another vision of her intellect, Dee boldly suggested that maybe if the patient was given some blood into his veins from another person that he might gain strength and survive from his very grave condition. And the priest was shocked to hear this suggested abomination, and he sternly pronounced that blood was a sacred substance and was only to be offered as a sacred sacrifice at the alter of the invisible god, and only then could some small amount of it be used as a powerful holy magic for healing when it was sprinkled upon those in need of the strongest sacred holy magic. And the priest most sternly reminded Dee that the use of blood for any other reason was denied by the written words of the invisible god's holy book. And Dee being strongly rebuked for her suggestion, said no more. And she watched in tearful silence as the wounded young man became ashen-white, and his young life expired, while the high priest reminded his invisible god of the faithful young soul, which was coming his way.

And it was a usual situation that within the Infirmary of Divine Mercy there were always many young bodies of those who were freshly dead, and who were peacefully awaiting there time for burial within some holy sacred ground, where at their grave side the priests would make a solemn promise to their unhearing ears that one day their invisible god would kiss their withered lips to awaken them to a new eternal life. And as forceful time pushed onward, it came to be that a new patient, a middle aged woman, came into the Infirmary of Divine Mercy, and Dee attended to this woman whose natural skin color was weak and whose body was weak and whose urine was dark as is strong coffee in its color. And the high priest came into the presence of this woman and he asked unto this woman what great sin she had made against the invisible god that she was cursed with such unnatural miseries. And the woman weakly replied, she had made no sin of her knowing against the invisible god. And the high priest said unto the woman that god would finally be the judge of what was of her own cause. And the high priest said unto the woman that in his great mercy he would perform the holy healing rituals, but it would be god's grace to decide the outcome of her situation. The high priest laid his healing hand upon the woman's head and he sprinkled holy water, and made ritual chants, and offered up sacred prayers and even burned incense whose ascending blue smoke would aid in carrying the prayers directly up to heaven's throne. And it happened that while the high priest was performing these holy rites of divine healing, a most powerful and insightful vision of intellect came into the mind of Dee, who having witnessed so much, for so long, had developed an instinctive eye which could see into the invisible causes and effects of many natural things, and while in a near trance-like state of her mind and of her vision, Dee suggested to the high priest that she felt that two bean like fleshy parts of the sickly woman might have somehow failed in their functioning, and that as an extreme yet hopeful measure that these fleshy parts might be replaced by the same parts taken from one of those dead but still warm young bodies that were awaiting their burial. The high priest upon hearing such powerful words, which suggested multiple blasphemies against the holy book's writings, threw up his hands and dropped his container of holy water onto the hard rock floor, and he turned and pointed his stern finger of accusation at Dee, who was trembling with fright, and the high priest said unto Dee, she was to immediately and without delay to report to the office of the high priest of the holy court.

And sadly in due time, after much holy deliberations, Dee was declared to be a blasphemer against the gospel truths of the sacred holy book and against the teachings of the invisible true god, and to this effect certain charges were made against her, and a time and place was set for her trial and her sentencing.

And as is inevitable the time set for her trial came to be at hand. And Dee was at holy trial accused of proposing that living bodies should be opened up to discover what causative agents of maladies might be there be found. And Dee was allowed some few words in her defense. The judges of the holy court said that the interpretations of the holy book forbid any opening up of a living body, and so her defense was denied.

And next at holy trial, Dee was accused of proposing that living blood from one person should be introduced into the veins of another person who was in need of blood. And Dee was allowed some few words in her defense. The judges of the holy court said that blood was the most sacred of all substances and that the interpretations of the holy book forbids every use of blood, except that it be offered up as a sacrificial offering at the alter of the invisible god, or upon occasions of special merit some of the offering of blood may be used as a powerful holy healing substance by means of sprinkling it upon the person in need of its healing power, and so Dee's defense was denied.

And next at holy trial, Dee was accused of proposing to cut into dead corpses and to by that means fiendishly steal from the holy dead bodies their sacred holy parts. And Dee was allowed some few words in her defense. The judges of the holy court spoke out with the greatest indignation against Dee, as their holy book strictly forbids the defiling in any manner a dead person's sacred holy body, and so Dee's defense was denied.

And next at holy trial Dee was accused of suggesting that parts from one holy body should be transplanted into another person's holy body. And Dee was allowed some few words in her defense. And the judges of the holy court covered their faces and moaned out loud mournful sounds that such an unholy crime could be suggested by even the worst of hell's devils, and they pronounced that the holy book's interpretations strictly forbids any and all transplanting of body parts from one individual to another, and so Dee's defense was denied.

And the time of the holy court's hearings and pleadings came to its end. And the holy judges of the holy court found the case against Dee in favor of the accusations, each and every one of them. And the holy judges of the holy court pronounced their unanimous sentence of death by means of cremating Dee's living body in public view that it would be seen as a symbol of what was the punishment to any who would blasphemy against the words of the holy book of their invisible god.

And it came to pass that within the public square, which was in front of the Infirmary of Divine Mercy was built up a huge pile of dried branches and wooden logs and at the pile's center was a tall wooden post to which Dee was firmly tied. And the peoples of the town came to the public square to see that holy justice had its place and time.

And the highest of the high priests brought forth the flaming torch of holy justice to set the holy fire to consume the living body of saint Dee Nighid. And the town's people celebrated holy justice by dancing around Dee's crematory fire, because in their great ignorance they did not understand that by their wanton action a powerful hope for their better future, was denied.

HID

And Hid being a person of a most contemplative and soul searching natural nature, was a person who often journeyed into the wilderness, where silence was abundant, and where her thoughts marched as the only lonesome voice in the hallways of her mind. And it came to pass that on a certain occasion, while Hid's thoughts led her on a journey through her mind, her footsteps led her, by their own sightless stepping, one-after-another, and Hid's walking feet led her ever deeper-and-deeper into the wilderness.

Hid was considering questions of deep substance, and she took no notice of where her walking feet were taking her. And Hid thought unto herself, why is it that people cannot share in the common communion of the sunrise as it brings peaceful warmth to the land? Why cannot children be raised in safety without their fearing the threat of nations or empires at war? Why cannot our kind find joy within the common laws of nature? Why from the dawn of recorded time has our kind's simple hopes for peace, friendship and happiness been always compromised by evil doings. Why is the future always portrayed as holding fearful things, which will be let loose as we arrive there? Why is hopeful change inevitably mired down in the mud of ever-fixed conservative traditions? Why do some persons diligently work at destroying what is new? Why is there no common communion between races, between religions, between different social stratums, between those with differing ideas? And why should ever, ever, the briar bush be made the leader of the trees? And then Hid suddenly stopped, for she had walked and bumped directly into the trunk of a knurled old olive tree. Her thoughtful questioning had been so all consuming of her mind's eye, she knew not, that she had been wandering in a vast grove of olive trees. And she knew not, how she had arrived there, but being a bit tired from her journeying, she sat down at the base of the knurled old olive tree and rested her back against the tree's broad and sturdy trunk.

And as she rested, there came upon the air the sound of voices. Hid peeked from behind the broad knurled old olive tree's trunk, and she saw at a little distance, a small group of children seated as a semicircle upon the ground. And seated at the semicircles opening was an old man, a storyteller, a teacher, and he was speaking with the children. Hid did not present herself to the group of strangers, but stayed behind the olive tree's great trunk, and from there she secretly listened to learn what it was, that was being said.

And the storyteller spoke saying, since long before recorded time, this kind of snake has lain hidden within the landscape. And one child asked of the storyteller, how did the snake get there? And the old man replied, the snake's very clever camouflage allowed it to slither unnoticed through time's evolution into today's landscape. And the children looked at each other, and wondered why they had not seen this snake. The teacher continued, children you must be very careful, for that very same snake has also slithered unnoticed into a different kind of landscape, a landscape not of rocks, grasses, trees, and forests, but into the landscape of our minds. And a child asked, how that could be? And the old man replied with a whispering voice, which was difficult for Hid to exactly hear what was spoken, but she thought the old man had said as a whisper, the snake is a spirit. And the children at hearing this, looked at each other with great curiosity, and one of them courageously asked of the old man, a good spirit—or a bad spirit? And the old man remained silent for a moment; he stroked his chin as if he was thinking of how to answer. And the children looked at him and wondered why he delayed in answering. The old storyteller took a deep breath and looking directly into the eyes of the child who had asked the question, and said, sometimes good, and sometimes bad, and sometimes very good, and other times very bad. And the children were all so surprised by this answer that no more questions came to their tongues.

Hid was tempted to call out a question, but she felt as a spy, because she was out of sight behind the olive tree and was eavesdropping on the group of strangers and their stories, and so because of these feelings, she was silent.

The old storyteller was himself silent for some time, but then he rose up and walked into the semicircle of seated children, and there asked of them, do you know of this spirit snake's presence? And the children looked at each other, to see if one of them would say yes, but no one spoke. The old storyteller stroked his chin and asked, have not you at some time been very angry with a person and struck out at them? And the children brought to their mind's eye, some memory of a time, when they had done such a thing, and they wondered if the teacher could see into their mind to see the images that were there, and so they were fearful to lie that their teacher had already seen the truth. And so the children slightly bowed their heads, and said a quiet, yes.

And behind the olive tree, Hid's lips spoke a silent, yes.

And the teacher again stroked his chin and then asked, have you not at some time felt sympathy for someone in distress and reached out to comfort them? And the children felt proud as they all answered, yes.

And from behind the olive tree, Hid's lips spoke a silent, yes.

And the teacher said unto the children, these are two different parts of the spirit snake that lies within your mind, one part is bad, and one part is good. And a child asked, is the spirit snake half bad and half good? And the old storyteller replied, the spirit snake has many different qualities, some good, and some bad, then he stroked his chin and repeated the words, many different qualities, and then he said, too many to say them all. And a child asked, does this spirit snake have a name? And the teacher smiled and said, yes it has a name. And the child asked, what is the spirit snake's name? And the teacher again smiled and said, the spirit snake's name is Instinct, and the spirit snake lives invisibly inside of all creatures, even within each and every one of you. And a child asked, why have you told us this tale of the spirit snake that is both good and bad. And the storyteller smiled a sincere smile, and said to the children, it is important that you know that the spirit snake is within you, so you can be the master of it, and it not be the master of you. And a child asked of the teacher, but how can we be the master of the spirit snake whose name is Instinct? And the teacher replied, you can become the master of all you behold, but you cannot be the master of that which you do not know. And the children were silent and they considered what the teacher had said. And one child spoke to the teacher and said, we are thankful you have told unto us this tale for now we can become the master of the spirit snake for we know it lives within us and we shall work to be its master and that it not be our master. And the old storyteller said, you are wise children, and it is certain you shall be the masters of all that you know.

And Hid stood from where she had been seated behind the knurled old olive tree and she hurried to depart unnoticed from the olive grove, lest the strangers become aware of her presence and by that knowing, become her master.

LIFE'S DREAM

The Great God of Creation dreamt a dream, which was the most powerful and promising dream of all dreams, a dream of contrasts so prominent, they each within their own domain pointed to the contrast of their opposite's domain. And by this simple yet elegant means one element enhanced the value and meaning of its opposite element. And by the force of the dream's axiom of opposites, all things began to have meaning, shape, and a substantial form of their own, yet somewhere with certainty was a balancing and opposing, opposite, and complementary form. And within such a simple duality of elements in opposition is contained the hidden majestic power behind all of creation. And by means of distributing each element's proportion within a mix, the delicate intricacies that lie between the opposing elements are defined, and the new mix gives variation its first truthful meaning. And within the dream, it is variation, which primarily fills what originally was a vast void. And the dream's most delightful and most promising variation is life. And all other dreams are as nothing, when compared to the most marvelous continuously unfolding dream that is life. Life's dream is of the sweet taste of honey and the bitter taste of poison. Life's dream is of the loveliest sounds of music and of the unpleasant sounds of racketing noise. Life's dream is of being with your lover and of having your lover forever lost. Life's dream is of comfortable warmth and of merciless cold. Life's dream is of the delicate flowers of springtime and of the final inevitable withering of their blossoms. Life's dream is of the light and of blinding darkness. Life's dream is of tasting cool pure water and of things parched dry. Life's dream is of health and of sickness. Life's dream is of wealth and of poverty. Life's dream is of freedom and of bondage. Life's dream is of gaiety and of sadness. Life's dream is of hope and of despair. Life's dream is of peace and of war. Life's dream is of love and of hate. Life's dream is of comfort and of pain. Life's dream is of good and of evil. Life's dream is of enlightenment and of stupidity. Life's dream is of youth and of old age. Life's dream is of happiness and of sorrow. Life's dream is of togetherness and of abandonment. Life's dream is of absolutes and of conditions. Life's dream is of truths and of falsehoods. Life's dream is of sanctuaries and of vulnerabilities. Life's dream is of sympathy and of unpitying. Life's dream is of excitement and of tedium. Life's dream is of saints and of sinners. Life's dream is of progress and of regression. Life's dream is of life and of death. And Life's ultimate dream is just to live and to savor all that is there to be savored, and to ever make the goodness of life's dream, stronger than the bad.

THE TREE OF KNOWLEDGE

I say unto you, the peoples of my new tribe, for our peoples to live in harmony and to have common mutual understandings, which have the power to better bind together your strengths, you my peoples must have enough of a common education presented in a common language, so a major part of the information within your individual memories is similar, and therefore it is relatable and understandable to others. Only by the means of a common, worldwide basic education, conducted in a language common to all, can you accomplish the important goal of living together in a world where there is harmony and understanding between my peoples.

I say unto you, my people should soon build throughout the world our "Schools for the Future." as a means of giving to your children the best education that you can devise. An education devoted in part to the common needs and common interests as the basis for establishing a common communion between our kind. And a second part of the educational system must be devoted to helping students, as individuals, to seek out and to begin specializing in whatever subjects most stimulate their interests. It is an unforgivable sin for cultures and institutions to mold children into adults, whose only options in life are not options of the individual's choosing, but are those, solely of the educating system's design. This is an unforgivable situation, as it traps women and men within its invisible yet confining form, whose economic claws coupled with the jaws of social taboos tirelessly work at the uncomfortable soreness of their unwanted position, and this brings a painful torture to their daily lives from where they have few options for escape.

I say unto you, in the world of your future, you must cause it to be, that all children receive the very best education that you can conceive. A truthful education where no knowledge is hidden from anyone based on the false premise that some knowledge is inappropriate for certain persons, or certain age groups, or that some knowledge should be reserved exclusively for certain groups and excluded from all others. Such ideas of exclusion are all complete nonsense. And know you this; children of any age can decide for themselves what is of an appropriate interest for them. If a child is uninterested, then it is plain for you to see that this is so, and if a child is interested, that is also plain to be seen. With careful help and guidance there should never be areas of knowledge that should be restricted from anyone.

I say unto you, you must free yourselves from the prevalent and popularly misconceived idea that marijuana is necessarily evil, and is detrimental to your physical and mental health, simply because the majority of the population has been misguided into believing this is true. Even though governments have built costly internal empires to administer this propaganda of marijuana as an evil substance, and even though they have built up vast costly armies whose primary battle campaigns are to keep marijuana away from the general population, you should realize that what is, or is not popular, should not bear any weight towards determining the truth or falsity of this common belief. I say unto you, all naturally occurring drugs should not be blindly lumped together under the taboos associated with certain dangerous and highly additive drugs. Marijuana, instead of enhancing physical capabilities, enhances in many ways an individual's perception of both their real and their philosophical world, and often gives rise to new insights that enhance creative abilities. I say unto you, there are multitudes of institutions within societies that do not want, and have a great fear should any individual be able to see any part of the world in a different way than the way they have been institutionally conditioned to see it. And I say unto you, marijuana as a naturally occurring substance is capable of opening wider the windows of all of your senses for a period of time, and thus allowing you to see the world from different perspectives and with a different understanding, which is not otherwise available you. Seeing the real or philosophical world from a fresh new viewpoint, opens up your mind to new interpretations and new creations, because you will become temporarily freed from the overpowering fog of bored familiarity. A familiarity which lulls you into foolishly believing that you completely know all of the daily repeated hum-drums of life, and therefore there is no need for you to be bothered with looking at what might really exist, as compared to what you have been conditioned to believe exists. I say unto you, instead of hiding in fear from appropriately and moderately using marijuana, which can temporarily enhance your mental abilities associated with insight and creativity, you must be willing to seize every possible advantage for enhancing your mental abilities as a powerful means of adding to your knowledge and understandings of Mother Nature, and as an aid to our kind, by giving them some further advantage at both surviving in nature's never ending game of survival, and to enhance our understandings and pleasure for our own aesthetic benefit. And I say unto you, to temporarily broaden the abilities of your senses, your creativity, your pleasure, and your understandings, is not a sin upon an individual or upon society, but a gift, a gift that should be utilized to its best capability, and to our kind's maximum benefit. But I also say to you, there are always some few persons who will not be strong enough to control a moderate use of this normally beneficial natural substance, and they will need societies help, but it is quite certain that without this substances, those very same few would be in need of society's help, because of a multitude of other reasons associated with their lack of personal responsibility and control. And I say unto you, it is not the substance that rules the individual, but it is some lacking or skewing of an individual's internal world that willingly takes the substance as a hoped for relief from that which the individual has been powerless to solve. And the individuals who are in this category are in dire need of help, independent of what substances are available to camouflage their hidden needs.

I say to all of the peoples of my new tribe, you must learn in exacting detail were your kind, human kind, has as its place in the drama that is your history of evolving by the magic of my natural evolution. When you clearly understand the most beautiful, the most glorious, and the most holy drama of evolution, then will you be able to see the great importance of intelligently and creatively working in everyway to contribute to your health, happiness, and your hopes for a kind of immortality. These understandings will give you sound reasons for respecting diversity within your kind, and of working together in harmony towards your best goals.

I say unto you the people of my new tribe, logic is a basic spiritual substance, which exists in all things of my creation. And I say unto you, without logic my universe becomes a completely unknowable thing, without form, without image, without feel, without tastes, without odors, without sounds, and without existence of any kind or nature.

I say unto the people of my new tribe, educate your children, for it will give them the gift of eyes that can see further than to the end of the street where they live, eyes that can see beyond the horizon, eyes that can see into the rock of mountains, eyes that can see to the bottom of the oceans, eyes that can see into the depths of space, eyes that can even see into the hearts and minds of the people.

HEAVEN and HELL

I say unto you the peoples of my new tribe, any pathway, which can eventually lead to the gates of a real heaven, has its beginnings in the deepest depths of the past's chaotic hells. Your kind, in your journey from life's beginnings to becoming the creature you now are, has already passed through, and survived, the worse of what the darkest of hells had to offer up against your most primitive relatives and against you. You have, by your time of long patient and past sacrifices, proven your worthiness before the Great Creator God to fully partake of the fruits of the tree of knowledge, and to begin the holy work of fulfilling your sacred obligation to bring heaven into a real existence.

Your home here on this most magnificent planet Earth is the best heaven you might ever enjoy, and it is, for now, your only sure paradise. You need to work diligently at making this paradise even better than it is, because as history is your witness, your kind has ruthlessly ravaged every garden and every other creature of nature with which your kind has experienced even a passing casual contact. I say unto you, it is absolutely certain, if you keep your present way of dealing with nature, you will eventually ravage the planet to a point of no return, a place in time and situation, from which the planet Earth can never return to again being a paradise, or heaven, your paradise, your heaven. Then, what once was your best real heaven will drift into becoming the chaotic hell of its most distant past's beginning. Your kind has proven many times they have, from purposeful intent or inadvertently, been a curse upon the other life forms that have their own natural property rights on this little piece of heaven, this planet you share with them. It is time you started, with serious intent, to heal any wrongful damage your kind has previously caused to happen, and to work at making the planet Earth flourish as the closest thing to a magnificent real heaven that it can sustain.

I say unto you the peoples of my new tribe, with new knowledge you will begin to understand that there are no major cataclysmic forces within nature, which belong to any false hell's or heaven's sole prerogative to reign their terror upon you. And I say unto you, that nature's cataclysmic events are all situations of nature, whose string of causal effects can be discovered and known down to the finest details of their long gestation. You can with certainty discover their now hidden mechanisms, which will give you the power to banish the hells that volcanic eruptions, earthquakes, floods, and hurricanes are able without resistance to impose their hellish destruction and death upon your nations and peoples. I say unto you, that by knowing in exact detail the nature of the causal forces, which are the infant seeds of these catastrophic events, that knowledge will give you an advantage of predicting long enough in advance of their coming, and you can protect yourselves from the hell that these events are now free to wantonly impose upon your lives.

I say unto the peoples of my new tribe, parts of hell still exists in your world. In some places it survives in a few isolated sanctuaries within a society that is otherwise generally filled with opulence, but in some nations, hell is the every day rampant state of affairs for most all of the population. It is your duty, your sacred duty, to begin the slow methodical work of vanquishing all signs of hell from this Earth. I say unto you the people of my new tribe, the time of the old outmoded ideas of heaven and hell, whose invisible gates were above or below the Earth, should forever be vanquished to the realm of false mythologies of the past. Hell is a condition that you blindly allow to survive within your otherwise somewhat civilized world.

I say unto you the people of my new tribe, for your kind, the situation you are each confronted with, independent of whether you are rich or poor, or however you live and exist, that whatever it is you have in this life, it is all of any kind of heaven, which you may ever be fortunate enough to know. And whether you like it or not, even this limited personal heaven, for each of you, rich or poor, educated or ignorant, young or old, beauty or beast, comes to a final end for each of you with your death, and there is not now any magical mystical heaven after death, and so you had better hear my call to make, what ever little bit of the heaven you now have, into a better heaven for you and everyone; a heaven where death itself is finally banished by orders issued by the peoples of the new tribe of the good and real God of Creation. And I say unto you, the primary resistance to your eventually having the best of real heavens comes from those who are diseased with contagious poisoned minds. It is their disease, which blindly robs your kind of my holy tools of logical reasoning, the only tools that are surely able to help guide your way safely through an unknown, uncertain future. And I say unto you, the tools of logical reasoning, which in the hands of the many, instead of just the few, can stimulate vast multitudes of people into becoming creative thinking persons, and to cause all of your best dreams to begin to blossom. And I say unto you, when you are free to create, without threats of condemnation from the believers of ancient illogical dogmas, you will begin dreaming, discovering, and creating a better world than anyone could singly dream. I say unto you the people of my new tribe, when you are free from the ancient awkward illogical restrictions that reside within the darkest places of contagious poisoned minds, then the time will have arrived, when the gates to a real heaven are suddenly opened, and you will clearly be able to see the path that leads from heaven's gate to a real heaven, a heaven that is always better, than the best that you can dream. And I say unto you, know you this with great certainty, heaven is not a certain place, or at a certain time, or a certain way, but instead heaven is a pathway leading, from its first gates, ever forward through time unending, and its path journeys through ever-changing never-ending landscapes, whose substance is the ever-changing, never-ending, best of all you can dream.

THE COMMANDMENTS

THE WORDS OF THE GREAT GOD OF CREATION

I am alpha the beginning without end. I am the dream that dreams. I am within you, and you are within me, and we are one, the greatest one of all creation, and our names, which shall be spoken, are: God of the Earth, God of the Universe, Creator God, Great Creator God, God of Creation, and Great God of Creation.

And I say unto you the peoples of my new tribe, here are my commandments unto you, use them as succor for your spirit that they might give you guidance through dark times to your rightful place in a heaven that is the best you can dream.

C1. You have a sacred obligation to your ancestors, who have endured through the most difficult of past times, where they bravely struggled ever to survive, so that you could live in a new and better time, than was their time. Your scared obligation to your ancestors is fulfilled by your determination to ever survive and to ever strive to make tomorrow a better time so that the struggles and sacrifices, which your ancestors made in your behalf, shall not have been made in vain. Honor your ancestors and the powerful estates of knowledge they have passed through time to be delivered into your hands.

C2. You are responsible for the Sacred Gardens of the Earth. You are commanded to manage them with wise and good consideration for all living things found there, with no unjustifiable consideration given to one living thing over any other. This beloved Earth is my divine anomaly, a part of my dream that I have left drifting in its lonesome place, it is one of my flowers of incomparable beauty. It is a place of natural magic, glorious vistas, and the most marvelous of living things. It is your home, a magical bubble drifting through endless space and time. Be true to your responsibility to keep this commandment.

C3. You inherited instincts, which are buried deeply within your being and each one of them was necessary for your kind's survival against the past's savage battles within its ancient hells. Many of these primitive instincts are now only thorns embedded in your crown of reason, and those, which are clearly offensive to good reason, must be effectively controlled or subdued for the benefit of a peaceful and prosperous world. I say unto you, always remember your humble beginning was as risen up mud, you are not fallen angels, you are an integral and inseparable part of my natural world, and my best dream is that you shall rise up high, even to the best of your ideas, and even unto the distant stars.

C4. You are forbidden the eating of human flesh, as a food to sustain your survival, or for any ritualistic purpose. The eating of human flesh is forbidden even when human flesh is present as the only means for supplying nourishment for your continued living. If you, or your kind, have come down so low on the evolutionary scale that you are willing to eat the flesh of your own kind, then you deserve to perish instead of to ever survive. It is not for an individual to survive at any cost, which in the last has brought your kind up high on the evolutionary scale, but I say unto you, your kind is surely there because of shared immortal covenants, which by means of their nonmaterial spirit finally brought you fast out from the darkest of primitive times where some living things feasted upon the bodies of their own kind. Your immortal covenants between individuals binds your kind to honor one another as you honor yourself, and these covenants of honor and trust shall not be broken by consuming the flesh of an individual of your own kind.

C5. You are to reasonably limit the number of your procreations. The time has long passed when profusely procreating was a benefit for your survival within a savage natural environment, which took your off-spring as its rightful sacrifice. It is a sin to be fruitful and multiply your kind without logically thinking of the inevitable consequences for your children, for you, for your freedoms, for your good hopes, for your societies, for your environment, and for all of nature. I did not create you to live upon the heaps of your own waste. Nor were you created to live elbow to elbow not unlike primitive things that clump together. It is my natural law that over success in procreation will spring open nature's door of sever judgment and thereby to most severely correct this dis-obedience of my commandment.

C6. I say unto you, as all living things of nature must evolve to sur-vive the tests of nature, so must societies ever evolve and pass through different stages of their development. And I say unto you, know with great certainty, whatever exists as a condition within your societies, has its existence as a consequence of either your society's chosen design, or as a consequence of your society's neglect. It is long past time for your kind's societies to leave their old adolescent ways and struggles behind to the past. It is the character of your nations that they primarily deal with one another by means of bribes, blackmail, or by the threat or use of physical force, when instead your nations should be dealing with each other in terms of what might be best for all of their peoples. It is time your nations put these unwholesome adolescent practices aside, and they instead claim their place as new and adult societies, which truthfully work for the best interests of all peoples.

C7. You are to give the first priority for using the world's resources to providing the best educational system that can be devised, and to make the best education available to all children for their enlightenment, and for this purpose you shall levy a tithe on the resources of the Earth which are extracted or harvested for commerce, and this tithe shall be used solely for the purpose and benefit of educating the people. And this tithe shall free the peoples from having their personal properties taxed, which is an evil thing, and leaves the people always fearful that they never in fact own those things, which they have by their own labors paid for in full, and no part of which belongs to any government or any other taxing institution. The peoples must be freed from paying an unending taxing rental on those things, which solely belong to them. It is only by being free from the evil tax on their personal property that the people can feel safe in their ownership, and only then will the people be freed from the fear that their property is forever vulnerable to being confiscated by those who have no real claim of ownership to the people's property.

C8. You are to search throughout all of my creation to discover the insights, knowledge, and the natural magic, which require logic and reason as the key tools of discovery. Look also into my records of things and times long past, which I have saved for your discovery and enlightenment, they are my records of prehistory, and are stamped within the page-like layers of rock that have long and patiently been waiting for you to open them up and to discover the delights of their revelations, that you might more completely comprehend the glories of my creations.

C9. You shall bring forth from the peoples of my new tribe, an army of my living saints, researchers, who will relentlessly work to broaden the discoveries and understandings of every part, without exception, of all things of my creation.

C10. You shall bring forth a great army from the peoples of my new tribe, an army of my living saints, teachers, who will teach our children both facts and how to become more powerful at understanding ever more complex elements and their associated strings of logic, and to help guide our children in discovering and pursuing their best dreams of every kind, that they might happily broaden their knowledge of my great creation, and thereby give them the necessary tools for one day making their own contributions to a more interesting and satisfying life.

C11. You shall bring forth a great army from the peoples of my new tribe, an army of my living saints, medical people, who shall relentlessly strive to discover and implement the real magic of living nature's functioning that they might ever better apply that magic to medicating, and in everyway healing the maladies of your peoples, and to give sight to the blind, the ability to walk to those who have been incapacitated, heal those who have some crippling of their bodies or mind, to give again the blessing of natural hearing, to heal nerves and to restore their normal pathways and functioning, and to in everyway contribute to the blessings of life as they were originally best intended by nature.

C12. You shall bring forth a great army from the peoples of my new tribe, an army of my living saints, Artists, who are commanded to make contributions, by means of their unconfined powerful magic of artistic creativity, which shall help our people to better see, feel, and in every way to understand all things, and to use their creative magic to make the ethereal substance of pure dreams into prophetic realities that the people can rejoice in their being revealed.

C13. I say unto the peoples of my new tribe, of my Religion of the Future, construct within each of the major cities of the world, a "Temple of the Arts," wherein each individual Temple of the Arts will be facilities of the highest quality, and where each of the various arts will have appropriate space to exhibit their creations. Each temple shall contain individual theaters for presenting live dramatic and comic theater, dance, musical dramas, opera, orchestral presentations, and motion pictures. The temple shall contain restaurants, which offer presentations from the culinary arts. The temples shall contain retail shops, which offer for sale art in every medium in which artists create their presentations. The temples shall contain various accommodations, apartments for visitors, studios for the artists, facilities for utilitarian services, and other facilities as are needed to bring all into a harmonious integration. It must be a place where the people can visit and there behold the powerful magic of the artist's dreams made real. You should send messages out to the businesses of the world to come and to be a part of these Temples of the Arts that they might contribute to the temple's greatness and to have good benefit from their association. The architecture of the building and of the landscaping around the Temples of the Arts should be as a great tribute to the Arts. The temples shall include parking structures of a sufficient capacity to easily accommodate the temple's visitors and employees. I say unto you, use your wise judgment and make these Temples of the Arts a most desirable place, which are inspirational to the human spirit.

C14. You shall bring forth a great army from the peoples of my new tribe, an army of my living saints, creators of new technologies, who will construct the ever better devices and other means for satisfying the people's and society's needs and to give significant help in everyway as you make your journey to an ever better future.

C15. You shall establish two separate private associations, one for young girls aged from six years to twelve years, and one for young boys aged from six years to twelve years, where the needs of their deeply embedded natural instincts to have and share unique experiences with a bonded group of their own sex can be fulfilled. Subgroups of youngsters and adult guides from these associations shall periodically journey into those still primal natural places in the world to see, understand, and learn to appreciate the marvelous complexities of nature which will be unfolded there for them. This is the only sure way that the children of my tribe can begin to understand the real substance of the world of my Mother Nature and therefore come to more fully honor and respect how great are my creations. And it shall be the unbroken tenet of these two groups that the places within the wilds of nature, which they enter into and eventually go out from, shall be left in the same natural condition in which it was originally found, with nothing there changed from what it was before their coming there. And your are further commanded that subgroups, of youngsters and adult guides from these associations, shall regularly visit the various functional facilities of the sciences, the arts, and of technologies, that the children might gain a clear and direct understanding of the dynamics of their society's complex functioning.

C16. And I say unto the peoples of my new tribe, form yourselves into specific unions, groups of my people who have in common certain interests, or who are persons related by their profession. And these various different unions shall compete within the domains of their particular expertise at making beneficial contributions to a better life for all of the members of my new tribe. And, the unions are commanded to use logical and wise decisions to carefully benefit their membership and to increase their social and expert value to the tribe. And they are commanded not, either by the shear power of their numbers or by other means, to ever wantonly hurt society's needs in exchange for a sole benefit to their own members. You must make your journey to a better future, by journeying together in purpose, or you will make no journey at all, and the time for your certain end will always be at hand.

C17. You are required to use your understanding and knowledge to the best benefit of your kind, and also to the best benefit of the other members of creation, and to especially use your knowledge for extending life as a healthy, productive, and pain free time of continued value for your kind and for those other creatures that are your companions and friends.

C18. You shall make no laws or acts against the holy rights of the individual to freely express in any way their individuality, when their expression clearly does not involve the physical or mental harm of other persons and does not transgress against my commandments.

C19. You shall make no laws or acts against any individual's sacred and holy rights to determining solely for themselves the disposition of their living bodies or their body's embryonic seeds. An individual's choices in matters of their body's functions are solely their prerogative and are without sin or condemnation when their decision has been made with good and wise consideration of my commandments.

C20. You shall begin at creating and implementing an ever better plan, for a systematic expansion of your knowledge beginning first with yourself, then your household, your society, your nation, and the world.

C21. You shall take the vast amounts of information, contained in written, photographic, artistic works, and audio records of all kinds and from all sources, and convert it into various digital formats, and then to cause the information to be made available for the examination by the peoples of the world. And you shall cause to be translated into a common language those original materials of other languages, and by this means the languages from all times and of all peoples will be protected from being lost and to always be understandable, because of their relationship to the common language. You shall undertake the fulfillment of this commandment as a most sacred and holy obligation, for the information is itself like the beginnings, the first real birth, of your immortal spirit and its ethereal nature is the only legacy of your kind, which by its nonmaterial nature can circumvent biological evolution. The vast amounts of knowledge, which your ancestors have passed to you, is itself a magical instrument whose power knows no bounds, when you use it wisely. And the sum total of this gathered information shall be named Sacred Knowledge.

C22. You shall generate multiple copies of the Sacred Knowledge and each complete copy shall reside at distant locations established at different holy sanctuaries, a sanctuary containing the Sacred Knowledge shall be located on each continent or within the major nations of the world, and these sanctuaries which shall be information storage and retrieval centers shall be made to connect to a world wide digital communications network, thus making the Sacred Knowledge available to the world and to render it safe from destruction and loss by means of its distributive locations. And the sanctuaries where the Sacred Knowledge is resident shall be named, Library of Sacred Knowledge, and the continent's or the nation's name where the library is located shall be attached to this name.

C23. You shall design new ceremonies for establishing holy and socially recognized bonding between two persons; ceremonies that are of significant meaning to any two persons who wish to have my tribe's legal and holy recognition of their mutual commitments to each other. Within these ceremonies shall be a part, which proclaims the sworn, and recorded, mutually agreed upon obligations of the two who are willingly bonded together as two united as one in their togetherness.

C24. You shall satisfy the now set aside instinct to groom those who you have chosen as your companions, friends, or lovers. This is an ancient instinct, which I have caused to be within some of my creatures, and which now lies mostly dormant inside of each of you, yet it is in need of being satisfied if you are to find contentment for its quiet yearnings. Therefore you should, when possible, and when you are privately with your chosen companion, friend, or lover, use some of this private time to massage' their body as a sign of your acceptance of them and for maintaining the establishment of your mental bonding with them, and this contact of your hand with their body will make a mark of satisfaction upon your neglected ancient instinct to mutually share grooming, and shall be as a holy sign that you are freely bonded to one another as companion, friend, or lover.

C25. Your shall not lie about another's acts, if the intent of your lie is to cause hurt either mentally or physically to another person, or to unjustly stain their character with what in reality is not there, or is of no business to others. If your lie is for the purpose of protecting or soothing some possible pain or suffering of another, then it is to be seen as a balm of kindness and sympathy, and if its foundation has within it only good intent, then it shall be said that you intended no evil.

C26. You shall respect an individual's holy right to communicate their personal understandings and their beliefs, and you should not take or make any action to silence them, or take or make a revengeful action because of the words that are communicated, if their message does not contain proposals of evil intent against my commandments, my people, or my tribe.

C27. You shall show respect to all of those persons who are members of my new tribe, though they be not kings or presidents or high up in any social hierarchy, for they are my people, who are civilized by their knowledge and their experience and have voluntarily recognized by means of their logical reasoning that they are a part, with you, of my new tribe, and even for this alone are they to be honored with your respect.

C28. You shall come to the best possible aid of any member of my new tribe, who is in need of assistance or of personal protection from any persons or groups that are of a threatening attitude towards one of my people. To assist and to save any person of my new tribe is to assist in protecting my and your kind's holy dream for an ever better future.

C29. Your commerce with others shall be made equally transparent to all those with whom you make trade, and you shall establish worldwide fair measures of the quantities and qualities of all items of trade and fair evaluations of the equivalence of monies and other instruments as they directly relate to the objects of trade for which they are offered as just compensation. And these relationships between the objects exchanged in trade must be made available, transparent, and understandable to any logical reasoning person who desires to know them.

C30. You shall honor and respect the many possibilities for experiencing the various sensual pleasures of your body, which you might personally discover are good, and which you naturally desire. They are many. They are yours to experience, and no personal faults or guilt of any kind has naturally been tied to any of them. You should never see any of the sensual pleasures as sins of the body, for they are my presents of holy joy for you, and as you partake of them, you should rejoice in the goodness of their holy nature. Care must be taken to experience the sensual pleasures with moderation that they do not become the idol addictions of your life to the exclusion of other valuable experiences, and these pleasures must be entered into with good judgment and consideration of their potential future consequences. You must take precautions that within the sharing of the sensual pleasures of the body that their elements of pleasure have not been somehow corrupted and then inadvertently consumed, or the corruption propagated to others.

C31. You shall not judge the nature of any individual because of any few physical or mental traits, which establishes them as belonging to a group that shares those traits in common. The peoples of my tribe, of my distributed nation, are solely to be judged and compared to others, by their works, their efforts, and their contributions for helping your kind to discover, understand, build, and to realize tomorrows that are ever-better for all of your kind, than is the world of today.

C32. You shall strive to make the supplies of foods and drink ever more safe from any and all sources of potential corruption, and all foods, which are surely known to be safe from undesirable contaminations shall be sealed and then marked with my seal as a sign that they are guaranteed safe for normal consumption. And anyone who by any means causes these marked and sealed commodities to become contaminated must pay the severest judgment in proportion to any harm they might have caused, or twice the judgment equal to whatever harm they cause. Food commodities which require protection from the natural temperatures of the environment, when they are known safe, must be sealed and marked with my special seal, which has the ability to record the evidence of their historical temperatures. The practice of irradiating meats should be encourage as a means of better guaranteeing the safety of the animal flesh you consume. Irradiated meat should be sealed and marked with my seal to indicate it has been made safe for consumption by means of my sterilizing radiation.

C33. You shall make buildings, which will be known as our new temples, solely and exclusively dedicated to be used by the peoples of my tribe, the peoples of my distributed nation. These dedicated temples shall at all times be open and available to the people of my tribe as a common place for their meeting, where they might at any time congregate within a relaxing and a most comfortable setting, where interesting ideas can be shared, discussed, and developed. Our new temples must contain the best facilities of many kinds to provide for my people's needs and for satisfying the various hungers of the mind and body including good food and drink. Our new temples must contain sanctuaries for both private and small group discussions, and wherein is provided the best communication facilities for communicating to any part of the world. For the peoples of my tribe there is not one certain day of the week which is marked over any other day as holy, for your kind every day is holy, and no one need call the people of my new tribe together to congregate at a certain time, or on a certain day of the week, a certain day of the month, or a certain day of the year. The peoples of my new tribe are free to congregate together at the time of their individual choosing, and therefore our temples must always be open and available to them. Inside each of our new temples shall be placed an alter of symbolic meanings. The alter shall consist of a wide low drawn earthenware glazed bowl, to symbolize earth, and the bowl shall be filled with pure water to symbolize the water of life, and at the center of the water filled bowl shall be an Eternal Ankh circumscribed by four individual flaming standards signifying, logic, reasoning, discovery, and understanding, and the flames of the four standards are symbolic of the flame of life, and upon the water of the alter shall be floated some few fresh flowers as a symbol for all living things, and the air that encapsulates the alter is symbolic of the protecting and life sustaining atmosphere of Earth. And whenever you come into our temple you should stand erect before the alter and make the toast which has been taught to you, and then drink a small taste of pure water which has been set nearby for you to drink as your sign of communion of understanding. Your are to set upon yourselves the responsibility to see that the alters within our temples are maintained in good condition as best they can be maintained. It is an honor to the peoples of my new tribe that smaller alters of the same design as those within our temples should grace your personal table where food is to be shared with friends and before eating you should sometimes offer the toast which shall be taught unto you.

C34. You shall make a small symbol which you shall wear upon your person as a sign to the peoples of my new tribe that you are one of their kind, a member of the tribe, and this symbol shall be as a sign of your personal commitment to our philosophy of logical reasoning, to our new religion, and as sign of your covenant with me, the Great God of Creation, and of my covenant with you that I am ever a part of you and you are ever a part of me. The symbol you are to make shall be an "Ankh," the symbol that for my peoples of ancient Egypt was their symbol for life, and the Ankh shall be resting its base upon the symbol, which represents the idea of infinity and eternity. This symbol is a representative sign for the dream of life eternal and of your commitments to making your world and its tomorrows ever better for all of the peoples of my new tribe within my distributive nation. This symbol shall be named "Eternal Ankh."

C35. You, my peoples, are free to celebrate whatever holidays are of your desire and to celebrate them in whatever manner is of your choosing, but neither name them or speak of them as the names they were given by the past's false religions, but celebrate the true pleasures of their time, and not the falsehoods that have in the past been intricately woven into their portrayals. You are commanded that when you are celebrating any holiday you offer up and drink a solemn toast saying, "We make this toast to the Great Creator God and to God's gift of holy logical reasoning, and give thanks for its enlightenment which guides us to a better future."

C36. You shall have one manner of laws that they shall be the same for all and not different for anyone, friend, relative, or stranger. The laws must apply equally and evenly for all, lest the laws be seen as not laws, but as favors for some and as punishments for others.

C37. You shall not steal what belongs to another person or is rightfully owned by others. The punishment for the thief who steals a material thing, shall be for the thief to return to the rightful owner the object which was stolen, and also one more of the same object, or some object or monies of identical value to the stolen object. All thefts shall cost the thief as proper judgment two to one of what was stolen and this value shall be returned to the rightful owner. The same judgment of two for one shall apply to thefts of every kind.

C38. You shall not kill your own kind without strong and good justification and reasonable proof that the act is done solely as an immediate protection of yourself or others who are in immediate danger of loosing their own life. You are given one exception within this commandment; in the time of war between nations it is reasonable that you use the best means available to quickly end the conflict with as few persons injured or made dead as you can reasonably control. And the peoples of my new tribe are to ever be powerfully vigilant at protecting the tribe and its philosophical doctrines and by every means to make the world safe for the peoples of my new tribe.

C39. I say unto the people of my new tribe, any person among you, who without doubt has been proven by the weight of logic and substantial evidence to be found guilty of murdering another person or persons, then those who are determined to be guilty of murder, shall have their name converted to an identifying number, and their living bodies shall be used anomalously in a pain free manner to aid in the discovery of medical cures that one day might be suitable to administer to your people in their time of medical need. Whenever one of these murderers dies, their body shall then be used by medical science in whatever manner they might choose.

C40. You shall not cut or maim your holy bodies, there are hidden future dangers from doing such things, but you can delicately pierce the lobe of your ears as has been the fashion since ancient times and is neither a sever deformity nor does it hold special unseen dangers to your future health. If you are in need of some bodily adornment then make that adornment from accessories of precious metals, precious jewels, or other artful works and wear them as objects, which do not penetrate through your flesh. The only allowable cutting into the flesh of the body, I leave solely to the holy realm of medical dissection of a dead body, or medical surgery, where surgeons work their training, knowledge, and technical magic to make wrongs, right, and to restore what has been taken away, or was naturally missing.

C41. You shall no longer practice the ancient ritual of religious or medical circumcision of either males or females, the severed parts of the body derived from such a primitive ritual are an abomination to me, and circumcision is a sin against those who have to go forth with such an unnatural marking upon their body. I say unto you, I know the people of my new tribe by what is within their hearts and minds, and I do not require a mark of any kind upon their body to know them one from another.

C42. You are to establish by means of election the positions of administrative authority that become necessary to administer the affairs of my new tribe, and to set persons into those positions of authority who have by a majority of the tribe's members been elected to those positions. No person shall be allowed to occupy any individual administrative position for more than five years of consecutive time.

C43. I say unto the peoples of my new tribe, give as your regular monthly sacrificial tribute to the tribe's common treasury, the amount your goodness of mind knows you might easily spare from your personal monies or other gifts. The wealth of the common treasury shall be used by your appointed administrators of these funds, to satisfy the needs of my peoples, the needs of the tribe and of my commandments.

C44. I say unto you the peoples of my new tribe, the administrators of the tribe's common treasury, shall make a monthly listing wherein each member of the tribe shall have their name recorded, and associated with their name shall be the amount of the sacrificial tribute they made to the tribe's common treasury. Also the administrators of the tribe's common treasury shall make a monthly listing, which contains the individual expenditures made from the tribe's common treasury and for what cause it was spent. These lists shall be available for any member of the tribe to witness.

C45. I say unto the peoples of my new tribe, obey my commandments unto you, for if you wantonly disobey my commandments, you shall be excluded from my tribe and shall be excluded from all benefits that are within the tribe's power to bestow, and you shall be shunned from having a friendship of any kind with any member of my tribe, and it will be forbidden for any member of my tribe to communicate by any means with you, you shall be as outside of and separate from my tribe. If you make sincere and substantial sacrifices and repentance for your disobediences to my commandments and make it published and generally known that you have repented and will henceforth obey my commandments, and if your pronouncements and sacrifices are accepted by your local administrators of the tribe, then you shall be conditionally granted to return to the membership of the tribe. And if you unwisely again disobey my commandments then you shall be excluded from the tribe with no recourse for returning to be again a part of my new tribe.

THE ARTICLES OF OUR CONVICTIONS

A1. We believe that no God, or Gods have ever before now, revealed a sacred divine plan for our salvation or given to anyone the keys to eternal life.

A2. We believe that the Great Creator God of the Universe does not intervene in anyway with the ever-unfolding dynamic majesty of God's Universal Plan.

A3. We believe that our daily and final destiny has, from our creation's very beginning, been and is our own individual responsibility.

A4. We believe the Creator God's Holy Plan is embedded within all of creation.

A5. We believe the Creator God's ultimate inclusive nature is beyond our present ability to exactly know and understand.

A6. We believe that the divine image of the Great Creator God is the image of the divine universe itself.

A7. We believe that the Creator God has never given the keys for opening the gates of heaven to anyone. The Creator God requires us to forge those keys.

A8. We believe the Fruits of the Tree of Knowledge are not forbidden by the Creator God, but instead, we are commanded to seek out those Fruits of Knowledge by every means, which we can devise.

A9. We believe the Earth is one of the sacred temples of the Creator God and each living thing found there is a representative part of the Great Creator God.

A10. We believe, for now, Earth is all there is for us of heavens or hells, and it is time we stopped trying to turn what is left of its heaven, into hell.

A11. We believe that to question the logical validity of any and every philosophy is our personal sacred duty.

A12. We believe the only trail that leads to the gates of heaven, passes first through the bowels of hell.

REVELATIONS

Blessed are those that read or hear the words herein written and who understand the logic of their meaning and their sure and certain prophecy.

Blessed are those who willingly protect and proliferate the substance of these writings to the others who also have rational logical minds.

Blessed are those who willingly and out of their love to see the best future, dedicate their life to serving the Great God of Creation, by diligently striving for ever better tomorrows.

Unto the reasonable peoples of the Earth, here are the revelations of the Great God of Creation, here is god's prophesied future, where hope is eternal and our best dreams become tomorrow's reality.

And your Great God of Creation speaks thus:

Unto the churches of the nations, behold my newly gathered tribe of peoples of great power and great understandings for they will bring forth new glories and fresh hope greater than all which has ever come before.

I am alpha the beginning without end. I am the dream that dreams. I am within you, and you are within me, and we are one, the greatest one of all creation, and our names, which shall be spoken, are: God of the

Earth, God of the Universe, Creator God, Great Creator God, God of Creation, and Great God of Creation.

I say unto you, the lamp of prophecy is reason, and there is no other light of greater illumination.

Unto the churches of the nations, time's passing has disclosed up and under your garments of power, is an evil body which dances a secret dance of eternal deception. In due time, you shall pay the terrible price which is justly proportional to your long unholy deceptions, your falsehoods, and the lie that you are holding the keys to heaven and hell, and the preposterous falsehood that you know the magic that can deliver life eternal. Repent now, for the time of your solemn certain and sure judgment is near at hand.

And to the people of my new tribe, who are a new and distributed nation, I give to them each a new name, which is secretly written, a name that collapses time and distance to their special advantage for establishing a shinning new communion with the others of their kind and who are of my new tribe.

And to the peoples within the world's nations, I give you a new time when every day is marked as holy, and no single day is set-aside for the mutual communion of our kind, but every day must be respected for our holy purposes.

And to the peoples of my new tribe, of my new religion of the future, a new church is given which is consecrated pure for it has no connection to those churches who have defiled and stolen my greatest of all gifts to the peoples. And my peoples have been commanded to make my new churches and my new temples. And the time is near when everyone shall receive judgment according to their true works.

Behold I stand at the door, and with the rod of reason I knock. Who hears my testament and opens their mind to its wisdom, I will come unto them and sup with them, and they with me, for our kind is one together, and we shall dine together in my churches and temples of enlightenment.

Behold those who comprehend my testament, they shall sit upon the throne of wisdom, and the glory of knowing the depth of my creations shall give them comfort in their times of need.

Behold the words that trumpet my prophesy of goodness for my peoples who understand, and who can begin to see the way to my promised future of renewed hope, where all things that I have created are there for their comfort and pleasure for which they have been justly created.

Behold, you have opened my sacred holy book, which has long been sealed by the master seal of time, and here, in my holy book bravely opened, see your promised future revealed, and give thanks for my opening of your eyes before death can steal your hope, your dreams, and your sacred future.

You will sing a new song, a song of truth revealed, and the number of those in the accompanying chorus who sing with you shall grow to become a mighty chorus, whose trumpeting voice shall penetrate even the rock of mountains, the ocean's depths, and throughout all the vastness of my creation. The song of truth will touch every creature, which is in the heavens and upon the Earth, and even those that are within the seas will hear the song of truth and it will bring benefit to all.

Some of my peoples will go forth, as if on a speeding white horse, conquering the beasts, which bring forth diseases and great sufferings to our beloved peoples.

Some of you, my peoples, will go forth as if on a speeding great white horse to bring my message of equal justice and peace to the world.

And some of you, my peoples, will go forth as a wind of mercy bringing sweet succor and nourishing foods to those of our kind who have great need.

Some of you will go forth to impede death itself and to heal the sufferings, which many times precedes unwanted death, and to nurture and comfort those who are in their time of great need.

And the sure and certain time will come, when my judgments fall heavy upon the heads of those who from the beginning of my creation have chosen to be deceivers, and to hide my truths behind every means of deception, which they could conjure up within their contagious poisoned minds.

And some of you will see into the depths of the Earth and see clearly the cause of earthquakes and give good prophecy of their eminent coming that our peoples might be saved from great sufferings.

And my peoples, by means of their secret names that bind them into a common communion shall be forewarned of nature's destroyers which might come as great winds, torrential rains, deep snows, huge icy hails, and even from volcanoes, and they shall be made safe from these forces of nature's blind fits.

And my people shall have a reward from their toil to bring forth good things from the Earth, and their fair reward shall be a most bounteous harvest in proportional return for their diligent labors.

And my people shall offer up the smoke of sweet incense and sincere prayers to my true saints, who have throughout time spoken the truth even when they were opposed by ignorant threats against them, and against their words of truth. Those whose lives were taken because they defended truth, they are my saints, my only saints, and they are worthy of your remembrance forever and ever.

And the trumpet of our united voices of logic and reason shall strike fear into those enemies who might think of trying to bring against us hail and terrible fire from the sky.

And to those who in sincerity attempt to assist, and to heal hurts they find in others, and then by their intended good service inadvertently cause more hurt, they are forgiven, as what transpired was from the best intentions gone astray, and no blame shall be on them as their hearts were pure and of good intent.

And you will squeeze, from the Earth's seas of salty water, fresh waters as pure as the purest of rains, and with your technology's magic the delicious water shall be delivered in gushing freshwater rivers to the places of its need. You will take some of the vast deserts and convert them into the most beautiful and delightful gardens, gardens whose glorious wonders are beyond what most persons can now imagine.

And the dark bottomless pit of ignorance and of unjustifiable fears shall be caused to be closed, and the holy light of enlightenment shall illuminate its cavity, and there to disclose its utter emptiness.

And the once blind plagues of creeping, crawling and hopping creatures shall be diverted away from my chosen peoples, whose strength is sacred reason.

And evil monsters whose substance is pure imagination shall be banished to live only in the realm of the world of dreams portrayed. And you will give to your new living bodies expanded senses for detecting, seeing, hearing, feeling, tasting, and smelling those now real but invisible wonders of the natural universe that bathe your unseeing spirit as you live amongst them unknowing of their ever-surrounding presence.

And your power shall not be from only the words of your mouth which have for the long past been used to speak poisonous lies, falsehood so weak of truth that only fools were made believers, but your power shall be stronger than all before, for its substance is derived from holy logical reasoning.

And you shall have the power to call forth rains in the time of your need. You shall have power over the waters that will dance to your tune and for your delight, pleasing you in everyway. And you will build public parks whose serene natural settings of plantings integrated with masterful monumental works of the Arts, will give a richer meaning to the emotional inspiration which love of nature can inspire.

And the time is soon at hand when the deeds of those who have been long gone shall be justly reviewed and their true names will be written within the book of true saints or within the book of the evil sinners depending on the judgments, and where they shall be known for time's eternity and the number of those greatest saints of all, shall be more than nine hundred and ninety-nine, more than a thousand, and even more than ten thousand shall be the number of the true saints of our kind.

You shall sing new songs and make new music whose powerful messages shall touch deeply, even to stir the holy emotions of my people's spirit. The future artists will give us new music of great depth of meaning and of new dimensions, which are capable of pleasing the ear's hearing and the brain's understanding to a level of pleasure and an emotional vision more than any power of the music of mystic sirens. Your new music will be as a triumph over your first music, whose only source came from the fierce pounding of your heart and the sound of your exhausted panting breath as it passed between your dry parched lips.

You shall come to comprehend the complete nature of plagues, and to set them aside; so they become beasts of the past and can have no further power over you. You will build a world where "Pain" and "Suffering" will be just distant fading memories of a human condition that once existed during a time long past.

You shall be healed and safe from all manner of sores and like curses, which have tried to creep unseen from the dark painful past, and free from unholy doctrinal cuttings, a common practice of times past, and you can be seen naked without shame in the full completeness of the naked beauty of your body, for it is completely a thing of holy beauty as I created it.

And the time shall be that women are honored equal to all others and seen in some ways as talented beyond most, a time when they will no longer be blasphemed for any of their womanly conditions, which I have made an inseparable part of them and which sets them apart from others but does not leave them as unequal.

And a great trumpet shall blow and choruses will sing of the restoration of the great cities of times past. Oh Babylon, and your time's great sister cities, shall in peace and harmony be reborn, resurrected and freed from tyrants of all kinds to again be the centers for the exchange of the merchandise of all earthly and spiritual things, which are most desirable, and your new glories shall out shine the best of your past. And the old and ancient major cities that time has decayed to the point that they are shame upon your character and upon your duty to respect the past's greatest efforts, they shall have back their old strength of spirit, and have a new life where they are technologically livable places within the grandeur of their original style. And my peoples will take those once great inspiring monuments left to us by the peoples of a history passed, and rescue them from time's decay, and restore them back to their original form and glory, that we might revel at the physical markers our ancestors left to us as a sign of their monumental struggle through time.

And you shall establish colonies of my peoples on the Earth's satellite the Moon. Colonies designed to become self-sufficient and to thrive as cities for nurturing human inspiration, creativity, and discovery. And in this distant and separated place, you will finally be gifted to see my great creations from a new point of view, a new perspective, which will give unto you a new inspiring vision for comprehending your place and destiny within the universe and the structures of my holy creation.

You will build a new world of personal transportation systems, which will make what you now have seem equivalent to handcarts and the animal drawn wagons of the past. You will build a new world, where any person, who by the efforts of their own labors and its benefits, will be allowed a passport, to travel to, or to live in, any part of the world that they might desire. And you will finally have your dream of personal travel to the most distant parts of the universe, and I say this promise unto you, the barriers of time will be without substance to hinder your voyages.

And no more shall nations and peoples be ruled and subjected to tyrants who wield rods of iron and whose stations of power are established upon the hurtful rocks of fear and the islands of potential eternal torment, but the nations and peoples shall be rightly governed by a system and its workings that are transparent to the eyes of the people, and where dark secrets have no place to be hidden.

And the time shall come for those who have been true to my throne of logic and my throne of reasoning that death will be banished and only to reign again by your individual personal decision.

You will build a world were your kind will make a new spiritual immortality, which can survive throughout all of time. And you the chosen peoples of my eternal creation shall have long life, and even life everlasting, as your choice, this is not given by primitive black magic, but by the divine magic revealed by the evidence contained in every atom, every rock, everything of every substance which are all the substances of my creation.

And you shall see and have a new heaven where the glorious words and works, of the trinity of true power, are named logic, discovery, and dreams, and there will flourish the very best of all you might ever dream. And in this new world, the words "Poverty" and "Unemployment" will be without demonstrable meaning. For there is vastly more good and necessary work at hand to be accomplished, than labor at any time can sufficiently supply.

And the goodness of what you have created shall heal the wounds of the world and of the peoples. And know you with great certainty that I am your Great God of Creation. I am Alpha, the beginning without end.

And these words you would be wise to capture within you mind and forever remember. Those seers of your future who looked out from ancient times were drunken with threes, sixes, sevens, and tens, which are the numbers of the unholy ingredients that have ever poisoned their minds and has caused them to see the future as upside down. Drunken by contaminated blood from black magic's veins, they have been led through a deceitful nightmare of fractured confusions and ever stumbling over the ghosts of their own wild imaginings. Their disguised insatiable lust for gold and precious stones exceeds that for the wholesome things of life even food, warmth, and sex. The have created a nightmare, where all great power resides within men, and the women are portrayed as a golden cup filled with abominations and the filthiness of their fornications, and who as whores led men to blasphemies and fornications. And these false seer's jalousies of any and every pleasantry have always been the foundations of their fortress of deception, fear, and hatred, and know you this with great certainty, the time of their deceptions is at its final ending.

THE END'S NEW
BEGINNING

Those of you, who understand what has been revealed within this testament, should intellectually bind together, for you are surely the Great God of Creation's chosen ones. You are persons, not belonging to one nation, and not belonging to one tribe, but are the ones of a new tribe, a kind of distributive nation united, whose inclusive boarders are those of a common understanding of what is here revealed. You are the only ones that together can forge the keys that can truly open the gates of heaven. To those of you who understand is given the responsibility to begin preparing the way towards an eventual time, when eternal life is our choice, and of giving a sacred birth to a new kind of life, a life which has always been nature's hoped for final product of all which has come before, a new form of life, which cannot be corrupted by the destructive elements of any hell's chaos.

0-595-26269-4